PRAISE FOR MOLLY GILES

Pitch-perfect in this stirring marriage of humor to heartache, the stories of All the Wrong Places hold up a mirror to the great, gaping maw of want and need at our very core. As a species, we can be a shameful, petty lot but the masterful Molly Giles has always seen—and shown us—more. This new collection is no exception: the wan and begging, the lonesome and disgraced, are made gossamer in Giles' care, made dazzling, transcendent even. Yet All the Wrong Places is no Pollyanna theme park; within each of these intrepid stories courses the truth of who we are, who we can be, and in all its clawing desperation, who we can never ever become.

—*Nicole Louise Reid*

You fall into Molly Giles' stories, and then you are tumbled around inside them, helpless to resist. Her stories spark right off the pages, combustive with wit and with sagacious observations. When you think you are laughing, you find you are crying, too. She writes with fierce originality and takes you deep into the minds and souls of her characters.

—*Toni Graham*

Molly Giles is a tough, brilliant writer who never is never afraid to confront dark emotions. Her stories shimmer with honesty. You will never be disappointed in the risks she takes. The narrators' spirit is both vulnerable and dauntless.

—*Thaisa Frank*

Molly Giles's stories are often funny, sometimes brutal, frequently both together. Quick and tough and oddly tender, burgeoning with strange, profound revelations, and strongly addictive.

—*Padma Viswanathan*

Molly Giles's exquisitely rendered stories are rare gifts. The stories in this remarkable collection are full of yearning and lost souls, outcasts and everyday saints. Her whip-smart prose and humor have won me over completely.

—*Melissa Cistaro*

ALL THE WRONG PLACES

ALL THE WRONG PLACES

stories by

Molly Giles

ACKNOWLEDGMENTS

Grateful acknowledgment is made to the following publications where these stories first appeared:

Blackbird: "Ghost Dog"
Cimarron Review: "Banyan"
Copper Nickel: "A Tale of Calamity"
Epoch: "One of Us"
Fairy Tale Review: "Kansas"
The L.A. Times West Magazine: "Five Minutes of Madness"
The Louisville Review: "Ram and Dam"
The Missouri Review and *O. Henry Prize Stories 2003*: "Two Words"
Narrative: "Accident"
Nimrod: "Mose in the Morning"
The Pinch: "Celtic Studies"
Santa Monica Review: "Fenced In"
The Southern Review: "Assumption"
Subtropics: "Give Me That"
White Whale Review: "Suicide Dog"
Witness: "Walking Tour: Rohnert Park"

FIRST EDITION

Cover Art: *Raise Above Drawing II* by Boryana Rusenova-Ina. 10"x10," watercolor, graphite on paper, 2013. This and other works by Boryana Rusenova-Ina can be found at boryanarusenova.com.
Author Photo: Stephanie Mohan.
Cover Design: Jess Bryant, Kyle Thiele, Nicholas Thomas and Caitlin Wheeler.
Interior Design: Erin Greene, Marie Hoffman and Dorian Karahalios.

LIBRARY OF CONGRESS CATALOGING-IN-PUBLICATION

Giles, Molly
All the Wrong Places/ Molly Giles—First Edition
pages cm.
ISBN 978-0-9908193-2-5 (alk. paper)
813'.54—dc23

2015003696

To Bridget, Nora and Danny, with love

TABLE OF CONTENTS

ASSUMPTION

MARY HAD HAD IT. The kids—kids?—Seth was forty and Stefani was forty-one—had been fighting since San Cristobol. *You are. I am not. Yes you are.* Cramped in the back seat of the rental car, Mary translated their back and forth invectives into Spanish for the softness, the quick prettiness of the language, but her pulse beat with impatience and her stomach started to churn. "Would you two knock it off?" she said at last. "This is supposed to be a fun trip."

"Mother," Stefani warned. Mary shrugged and turned her hearing aid off. Seth had a large grey mole on the back of his neck that trembled when he shouted, she noticed, and Stefani's cheeks were blotched with bad temper. They had been a beautiful couple when they first married, but they were a haggard, adulterous, materialistic twosome now. It was not her fault. Not her business.

You don't need a bigger car—Mary read Seth's lips as he turned in profile, mole bobbing, *You need a fucking U-haul*—and Stefani, equally unimaginative, replied, *What I need is a man who isn't a fucking miser.*

If we did nothing else right, Mary thought, Stefani's father and I knew how to fight. Didn't Stefani know that Seth got a *deal* on this rental car? Didn't Seth know that Stefani *shopped*? Mary sat jammed among garden urns, a wrought iron wine rack that had been torched to look rusted, a pile of woven rugs, three hammocks, and several extremely sharp-edged tin mirrors that, stacked in the seat beside her, reflected her face upside down, doubling her double chin and the bags under her eyes. She regarded her reflection, remembering the handsome old boatman who had given her a wink as he oared her and the kids through a lake strangled with floating lilies at the resort last night.

She turned to the window. The mountains in this part of Chiapas were an exquisite blue. The air outside, she thought wistfully, probably smelled of wood smoke from dinner fires, small good dinners of roasted corn and chicken marinated in limes and chilies—she'd never know, because Stefani insisted on windows up, a/c on. Speeding, Seth swung around stocky Mayan women in embroidered blouses walking single file along the edge of the forest, dark-faced men bicycling back to their villages. Every now and then a few shacks appeared and disappeared. Mary waved to the children standing in their dusty yards with their dogs and their pigs, but they didn't wave back—why should they?—just another old American lady, passing by.

Her stomach gave a decisive lurch. "I'll need a bathroom soon." She could never tell how loud her voice was with her Telex off; not very loud apparently, because neither turned to acknowledge her, though Seth, scowling, waved toward the scenery as if to say: No gas stations, no towns, no bathrooms. The road curved and wound, around and around, into the clouds. Mary rubbed her belly and sat back. She had always loved car trips; she was a good traveler. San Cristobol had been her favorite city so far, and its cathedral, where, kneeling, she had celebrated the Feast of the Assumption that morning with beautiful brown skinned women in brocaded *huipils*, men in pink *serapes*, businessmen in polyester shirts, teenaged soldiers, children, and a van load of chatty French tourists, had been her favorite place. But some fruit she had bought from one of the shawled vendors on the cathedral stairs was not setting right. She could feel an evil fluid begin to burble and bounce inside her. "I'm getting sick," she announced.

I told you not to eat those plantains. This was Stefani, mouthing. *They were fried in pig fat but oh no, you had to have them.*

"They were delicious," Mary explained. Stefani winced and sat back, and Mary, hand pressed to her abdomen, winced too. The plantains had not been delicious. They had been green and greasy and she had only eaten them to spite her know-it-all daughter who had eaten nothing but protein bars since Merida. She had been an idiot to bring Stefani and Seth to Mexico. Just because she had had the happiest years of her childhood here—years ago—did not mean that they would enjoy what she enjoyed: the soft warmth of the mountain sunshine, the earth colors of the sky at dawn. She smiled, remembering the lively community of expatriate artists her parents had reared her in. It was a childhood of flowers and fountains and fiestas, and she would trade it for nothing. She snapped her hearing aid back on and leaned forward, hoping to distract the kids with stories of her happy early life but a new stomach cramp stopped her.

She pursed her lips and pressed her buttocks together, trying to suppress an insistent fart, but it exploded anyway, and she watched as Seth and Stefani turned to accuse each other and then, in a helpless rush of shame, she felt her bowels loosen altogether and flood her jeans and the scratchy woven rug she'd been forced to sit on for lack of room. Horrified, she tipped her head back and closed her eyes.

"She's dead!" Stefani cried.

Oh honestly.

Still, it was a good idea. Mary kept her eyes closed.

"The smell!" Seth swerved so that one of the mirrors tipped and scratched Mary's arm. "I can't take the smell."

"My mother's dead and all you can think about is the smell?"

"I don't like the smell of dead people, okay? Is that okay with you? It has nothing to do with your mother, per se."

"Per se? Excuse me? This is my mother we are talking about!"

"Well what do you want me to do? What are we going to do? Tell me what to do."

"We have to find a hospital."

"How?"

"I don't know! We need to find some Mexican and ask for help."

"We don't speak Spanish. Only your mother speaks Spanish."

"Only my mother *spoke* Spanish." Tears. Then, "We're in the middle of nowhere."

"I really cannot stand the smell."

Brakes. Seth throwing up by the side of the road, Stefani begging him to pull himself together. Mary opened her eyes. It was dark. She was surprised. She wasn't aware that much time had passed. Maybe she really was dead. But no. She could smell herself. It wasn't that bad. Just natural human shit. It didn't feel that bad either, cooling around her ass and thigh like a mud bath in a spa. Still, it was humiliating. As old age was humiliating. As being in the back seat with children in charge was humiliating.

"I can't drive with her in the car," Seth said.

"We are not going to leave my mother, who paid for this trip in the first place, if you will recall, dead by the side of the road."

"I was thinking," Seth, humble, low, "we could strap her to the top of the car."

"Do what?"

"Wrap that rug around her and strap her on top. Until we get to a phone."

Silence.

"Until we find a hospital."

Silence.

"It's the only way I'll be able to drive, honey."

Mary opened her mouth to scream a protest but nothing came out. Stunned, she made herself still and stiff as the corpse she was supposed to be, as, nagging and gagging, the two people she had once loved more than anyone in the world wrapped her in the rug, hoisted her up, and strapped her to the roof with rope from one of the hammocks. When they got back inside the car and began to drive she opened her eyes and stared up at the stars. She could smell the smoke now and the deep smell of the pines and feel the cold fresh wind. She had never felt so free, so lonely, so invisible or so angry. Below, she knew her daughter and son-in-law would still be fighting. They had fought over the house she had bought them, the dental work she had paid for, the debts she had settled. They didn't mind fighting. They liked it. They probably even liked each other. I'm the one they don't like, Mary thought. I'm just an inconvenient old lady with a convenient bank account. She began to cry, then let herself once again be taken by the beauty of the night sky above her, and eventually, despite the irregular jolt of the car beneath her, she fell asleep.

When the car braked, she awoke. Struggling up, she saw they had stopped before a dusty little outpost sitting all by itself at the edge of the forest, lit up like Christmas with green and red bulbs. She heard the kids dash out of the car and run toward it. She would wait until they returned and then she would confess and tell them the truth and they could all fly home and put this nightmare behind them.

But minutes went by. And more minutes. And more. Finally Mary untied the hammock ropes and sat up. The front of the *tienda* was stacked with the bright woven tapestries Stefani had been looking for all week. She's shopping! Mary thought. Damn her, she's shopping, and Seth is haggling, and they'll be in there for hours. She slipped down the side of the car, into the driver's seat, pulled the extra set of keys from the glove compartment, started the engine and drove off. She did not permit herself to laugh for miles, but once she started, she could not stop. She could picture the kids when they came out and found the car gone. They'd think "some Mexican" had stolen it with her dead body on top. They would start to argue about whose fault it was.

Mine! Mary thought exultant. Mine, all mine!

She'd give anything to see their faces. But that was the trouble with being dead: You couldn't hang around and enjoy things. She'd just have to head back to the resort with the lily lake, clean herself up, buy some pretty clothes, and find that good looking boatman. Then she'd call her lawyer back in the States, get her will changed, buy a house up here in the mountains and settle down, at last, to the life she had always meant to live.

TWO WORDS

Roy got up at five to start cooking for the firemen. He had been getting up at dawn for weeks now anyway, ever since the last seizure, but usually he just read his affirmations and practiced Tai Chi in front of the turned-off television set. Today he wanted to talk. He couldn't wake Jill; she needed her sleep and, as their marriage counselor had pointed out, she also needed plain and simple "time out" because Roy (and Roy knew this, and was sorry) was driving her crazy. So Roy slipped out of bed and went to his daughter's room. Baby Tess lifted her arms and allowed herself to be carried to the kitchen but she squirmed and covered her ears with her blanket the minute he opened his mouth, so Roy had no choice but to address God as he understood Him.

Or Her. For Roy's God was a girl, about twelve years old, slim and lazy with lit dewy eyes and sharp little teeth. She could be generous and fond one minute and casually vicious the next. He had felt Her sour breath on his neck since his childhood but had only named her God and honored Her as such since the diagnosis of his brain tumor six months ago. By trial and error he had also discovered, at about the same time, that the best way to treat Her was with extravagant respect. No matter how badly She herself behaved, God expected good manners from him. She especially liked to be thanked.

Thank you God, he said silently, sitting naked on the kitchen floor among the tumbled cookbooks with his palms turned up and his closed eyelids jumping as fast as his pulse, *for all the people I've known who are up there with you now, including* (he counted) *mother, father, stepmother one, stepmother two, and Leslie, poor Leslie. May they be filled with loving kindness. And in the meantime thank you for keeping me away from them and letting me live a while longer. Thank you for the Zen Center, the Positive Center, WellSpring, Spirit Rock, and Esalen. Thank you for chemo and radiation and antidepressants and aspirin and medical insurance. Thank you for all the doctors, even the last one.* He paused and passed one hand over his bald head, pleased as always by the plush resilience of skin over skull. *Thank you for giving me a nice round head. Thank you for making it the color of mozzarella.* Thinking of mozzarella made him remember the lasagna he had promised the firemen. *Thank you,* he finished, palms tingling, eyelids twitching, Baby Tess poking at the dragonfly tattoo on his thigh, *for helping me find the right recipe.*

He had spent the day before at the library, going through cookbooks. He had explained to the librarians that he wanted a recipe that was saucy and cheesy and rich, and it was astonishing to both him and the three helpful women how many so-called good cookbooks called for low-fat cottage cheese in place of ricotta, yogurt in place of white sauce, ground turkey or even sliced zucchini in place of sausage and beef. Some chefs used no salt; others boycotted butter, and none gave directions for making the noodles from scratch. He had no luck finding the recipe he'd used as a boy, working alone in his father's bachelor apartment, but Martha Stewart, of all people, had a cookbook that offered a passable compromise and if he combined it with recipes from four other books, he knew he'd have a killer sauce, fit for his heroes.

"Roy!" Jill said, coming into the kitchen. "What are you doing?" She stopped. The marriage counselor had told her not to assign blame. "Are you all right?" she asked, her voice intent on softening.

"I'm fine." Roy opened his eyes, flexed his palms, and smiled. He always smiled when he saw Jill. She was so pretty and young and quick. Her eyes matched the blue of her bathrobe, the blue of the ribbon around her long drooping pony tail. She was the best thing that had ever happened to him, he told her that all the time, and at first she used to chime in and say No, *you* are the best thing that has ever happened to *me*, but she didn't say that any more. "I knew there would be problems," Jill had told the counselor—last week? the week before?—"I mean, he is ten years older and had been married before and then widowed and he already had Baby Tess when I met him, but I never thought there would be problems like this. I never imagined this."

Who could? First the trouble with his balance. Then the memory loops. Handwriting shot. Headaches like train wrecks. "And now," Jill had said, "I have two children. Two children and I've never even been pregnant!" She'd started to laugh but then she'd burst into tears and Roy had sunk into a ball, right there on the counselor's carpet, curled up, hugging her ankles, rocking back and forth, crying too, so sorry he'd done this to her, so sorry! Until at last she reached down and said, "It's all right." But it wasn't. It couldn't be. What had he cooked for poor Jill on their first date? Wild duck? Truffle risotto? The road to hell, Roy thought, is paved with food inventions.

Thinking of food made him jiggle Baby Tess off his thigh and hand her to Jill who cupped her up incompetently and stood looking at him. Beauties, both of them. "I'm a lucky man," he said, as Jill carried Baby Tess back to her crib. He waited until the dizziness sank and he was sure he was not going to keel over, then tied an apron over his bare belly, found his reading glasses by the phone and opened the cookbooks to all their marked places. Make the noodles first. Then the three sauces. Assemble. For dessert, good vanilla ice cream, fresh strawberries, and the same chocolate chip cookies he'd made for the delivery boy after his first seizure, when he'd writhed in the rain in the middle of the street until the pizza van braked for him. He could still hear the boy's high, astonished voice. *You're fucking lucky to be alive, man. You're a miracle, man.* And he was. Nothing but a bruised hip from that one. And other miracles followed. A dislocated shoulder from a fall in the shower had been fixed with one good whack from the chiropractor. A tumble off the roof that should have broken his neck only banged up one knee. Jill had yanked his arm back in time from the garbage disposal. God had screamed "Truck!" in his ear the last day he'd driven. He'd swerved off the road and though he'd cut his eyebrow on the steering wheel, there was no mark now. Odd the parts of the body that decided to heal, while the tumor wavered, shrinking and then swelling again, capricious. Five years, one doctor said. Five minutes, the last one had said.

He shook out his morning dose of deadly meds, swallowed them down with Willard's Water, and began to measure out flour for the pasta. After awhile, excited by the elasticity of the dough beneath his hands as he kneaded, he forgot his promise to be quiet if he got up early, opened his mouth, and started to sing.

Jill heard him but she wasn't mad. She smiled when she came back in to make coffee, a slight smile, not granting much, but enough to let him know that the sight of a bald man draping noodles to dry over the backs of kitchen chairs dressed in nothing but an apron and a tattoo while singing "You Are the Sunshine of My Life" was all right, was fine, was funny, was sweet. She had not smiled at all last month—was it last month? month before?—when he'd risen at dawn to rearrange the living room. She had not liked the Feng Shui; he'd had to put everything back. She'd been upset when he'd cut the plum tree down—it almost fell on the house—and after he'd pulled the carpet up to expose the genuine, if battered, parquet underneath, she'd forbidden him to refinish the floors. But since the last seizure, on the hiking trail, she'd been gentler. And now, as she opened the refrigerator for milk, saw the packages of ground beef and Italian sausage he'd forgotten to add to the tomato sauce, she was almost as upset for him as he was for himself.

"I want the firemen to like this," Roy explained, fighting tears as he sautéed more garlic and added the meat. He leaned over the flaming pan and tried to kiss Jill on the cheek. She gasped and reached for the handle in time. "I want them to like *you*," he added, chastised, moving back as she waved him toward a chair. "I want one of them to like you a lot."

"You're not making sense," Jill sighed.

She said that often.

But she was wrong.

"You can't really be mad at him." He heard her on the phone later that day as he was painting Baby Tess's toenails. She'd wanted blue. "It's the medication he's on. They change it every week. They don't know what they're doing." He blew on Baby Tess's toes until they were dry, then fit one fat foot into a new red sandal.

"Ready to walk to the store?" he asked.

"No," Baby Tess said. "Park."

"Okay, we'll walk to the park."

"No," Baby Tess said. "Store."

He looked into her fierce eyes. "You are just like your mother," he revealed. Baby Tess, who had never known Leslie and thought Jill was her mother, raised a fist and he kissed it.

"I'll say one thing about those fireman." Jill paused. He could actually hear her lick her lips across the length of the room. "Eye candy. Total eye candy."

Good, Roy thought. He smiled as he fit the second sandal onto Baby Tess's foot. So Jill had noticed after all. He just hoped she'd noticed the right one. Two of the firemen had given him CPR, two others had carried him down the hiking trail on a stretcher, but it was the tall strong one who had stayed with him in the ambulance, soothing Jill in a deep voice, that he was counting on.

Stu. The chief. Roy pulled on his beret and followed Baby Tess to the front door. "Bye, love," he called. "We're going to the store." Baby Tess opened her mouth to scream. "Park," he amended. "I'll be back in time to make the cookies." Jill, on the phone, giggled throatily, ignoring him. Am I jealous? he wondered. He shut the door and trudged down the driveway. He hoped he wasn't jealous. It was all right for Baby Tess to be like her, but he himself did not want to be like Leslie.

Leslie. His first wife. The one who had died. Leslie's last days had been so miserable that Roy had taken them to heart as life's lesson. No whining for him, no complaining, none of that Why Me—it just made things worse. Who knew why God dumped a bucket of bad luck on one person and slipped a promise ring onto the finger of another? It made no sense. Leslie had had a grotesque life. She'd been orphaned as a baby, abused as a child, abandoned as a teenager. He'd been thrilled by her nervy blonde looks and her easy, articulate self-pity. He'd cooked—what had he cooked for Leslie on their wedding night?—rack of lamb in pomegranate sauce? And then, with no warning, she'd been stricken with a rapid, debilitating, and very rare form of paralysis. It was a joke; it was no joke. The pregnancy she refused to terminate was a horror; she was blind, crippled, furious. She blamed him; she blamed Baby Tess. She sat in the dark and begged for a gun, over and over, *just get me a gun, goddamn you, do something right for once.* She'd probably be deeply gratified to see what had happened to him now. She'd probably say, *You see? I was right. No one escapes. Not even you, Mister People Pleaser. Mister How Can I Help You. Mister Totally Useless.*

He nodded to Mrs. Holst, who lived across the street, and stopped, Baby Tess yanking hard on his hand, to talk to Old Ed, the neighbor on the left, about the new stop sign. Was it a good thing? A bad thing? A good *and* a bad thing? Gypsy, the Brogan's dog, met them at the corner and was soon joined by Marcus, the Klein's lab, and Flip, the Legaspi's mutt. "We are leading the dog parade," Roy said to Baby Tess. "They want to go to the park too."

"Store," Baby Tess corrected, but the minute he turned toward the store she steered him toward the park, where he happily spent the next hour—two hours? half hour?—pushing her in the swing, throwing sticks for the dogs, digging in the sandbox for China. When he came home, the house smelled like chocolate—Jill had gone ahead and baked the cookies for him—and there was time for a bath and a nap before they drove to the firehouse. There was even time to paint his own toenails blue.

The firemen were waiting at the firehouse door, seven of them, maybe not "eye candy," but good looking men nonetheless, better looking than Roy had been in his prime. Stu in his crisp uniform introduced the others: Scott, Skip, Steve, Stan, Scott Again, and Sam. They ranged in age from twenty-one to about sixty, but they all had thick heads of hair, wide shoulders, and open outdoorsy faces. "I salute you," Roy said, shaking hands. "You are my heroes." Stu laughed politely; he probably heard that all the time, but a few of the other S's gave him strange looks. Roy knew what they saw: a puffed pale freak with wide lit eyes whose life they had saved once and might need to save again soon. Until then, a voter. A homeowner. Proud father of a cute, if clingy, little girl (Baby Tess was clamped around his neck) and a pretty, much younger wife. Jill had washed her hair and released it from its ponytail so it waved over her shoulders. She was wearing rose perfume and slick brown lipstick. Two of the firemen helped Roy carry the foil-wrapped casseroles, the garlic bread, and the salad in from the car. Places were already set at a long table in front of an enormous television set. The baseball game was on and Jill asked intelligent questions about it. Roy did not care for baseball but he chuckled attentively as one of the Scotts reported on the inning they had just missed.

Stu gave them a tour of the station before dinner. Jill admired the new computer system while Roy studied the huge county map on the office wall. "This is where you found me," he said, pointing to a dotted hiking trail. "I won't let him walk there anymore," Jill chimed in, sounding authentically wifely. "Now I just go to the store and the park," Roy agreed. "Hospital," Baby Tess offered, lifting her head off his neck, her first word in an hour. "But we drive him to the hospital, honey," Jill explained to Baby Tess, "he doesn't walk there." "That would be a long walk," Stu said. Strong chin. Strong back. Ringless. Roy smiled and moved in.

"Jill is a wonderful woman, isn't she," he said, "beautiful, the best, and Baby Tess, what a darling. And you know what?" He looked up into Stu's clear hazel eyes. "They would be all alone now if you hadn't helped me."

"That's our job," the firemen said, all of them, one after the other, looking neither pleased nor puzzled, just matter of fact.

"Well it may be your job," Roy continued at dinner, "but I want to make a toast anyway." He stood and lifted his plastic glass of lemonade to the table. "I'm only sorry this isn't champagne," he began. "Or," amending that at the sight of the flat polite looks that met him, "beer." The men relaxed and smiled. He was glad to see they had all helped themselves heartily to lasagna and bread. "It's a crazy thing to bring dinner to the world's greatest cooks—everyone knows firemen are the world's greatest cooks—but I've been cooking since I was eleven (I used to cook for my father after he left my mother—that's how he got women, my father, and what a miserable lot he got, poor guy, he'd bring them back to the apartment and I'd cook for them—you might say my brisket cooked his goose) anyway—I know, honey—" to Jill—"I'll get to it. The thing is, I couldn't think how else to say thank you. I wouldn't be here tonight if it weren't for you guys. You saved my life and I just wanted you to know how grateful I am. That's it. That's all. Just thank you." He put down his glass and clapped and Jill and then, surprisingly, Baby Tess, clapped with him.

The firemen waited until Stu said, "Sure, no problem," and then they all ate and the conversation turned to jobs in general, Roy telling them how he thought his old job in sales was probably the reason he had the tumor in the first place, all that getting up and getting dressed and getting out every day when he never, not once, wanted to, and Stu, smiling at Jill, saying there wasn't a day when he didn't feel happy to go to work, and Jill saying she was lucky to be able to work at home now that Roy needed watching, and one of the S's saying he had once, years ago, thought of being a policeman instead of a fireman.

"Oh but that's a dirty job," another S said.

"The things you see," another agreed.

"Makes you hate human nature," another said. "Makes you mean."

"Policemen are mean," Roy agreed. "When my wife—my first wife, that is—died, a bunch of policemen came to the house. They . . ." he trailed away, stopped by Jill's curious look. He had never told her about Leslie's suicide. "They didn't come to help," he finished. He was glad when the S on his left asked about the lasagna recipe. The mention of Martha Stewart silenced everyone, then they recovered to talk of other entrepreneurs, stock tips, day trading, hobbies, sports, fishing, all interlaced with the shy references Roy had become used to about various bizarre illnesses and, as always when talking to other men, hair styles. No one mentioned baldness, but it became clear from some clannish laughter at the end of the table that Stan used Grecian Formula and that Skip had a hairpiece. Stu could not bear to have his hair ruffled and Stan had a special comb no one else was allowed to touch.

"Is this what you do when there aren't any fires to put out?" Jill asked, sparkly. "Pick on each other?" The men laughed, blushed, hung their handsome heads. The casseroles and salads went around and around, followed by the cookies and ice cream and fruit. No one would let Roy clear, and although Jill tried to do the dishes, the men marched by her one by one and rinsed and loaded their own plates into the industrial sized dishwasher. Roy crouched with Baby Tess by a whiteboard on the wall, helping her draw a wall of flames with colored chalk. He heard Jill from the kitchen talking to Stu in the same dramatic low voice she used at the marriage counselor's. How pretty she looked. How easy it would be. He'd simply invite Stu over to check the firebreak around the house next week. Leave an apricot pie on the counter to cool, make a pot of fresh coffee, and then take Baby Tess on a long walk; they'd go to the park *and* the store.

He straightened, tired. Jill saw his drained face and made their goodbyes and they left with their clean dishes, everyone waving. "Glad to see us go," Roy said, cheerful, as he sank into his seat in the car. "Now they can be themselves again."

"Oh I don't think so honey." Jill drove with both hands on top of the wheel. "I think they had a good time. That fire chief, Stu, told me hardly anyone ever thanks them. And that's a shame."

"It is," Roy agreed. He closed his eyes. His father had never thanked him for those two stepmothers. Well, who would. Leslie had never thanked him either. "The thing we don't understand," the policemen kept saying, "is how she managed to get hold of a gun. Blind and in a wheelchair? How'd she get a loaded gun?"

It would not have taken much on Leslie's part. She had time. He'd left pen and paper beside the revolver. A short note would have done it. Two words. But no. Leslie never had manners. Forget it, Roy thought. It's over, it's done with. He felt God come down, heard Her hot little giggle, felt Her fingers, sharp and pointy, start to twist his skull as if it were the knob of a disliked doll. His head rose toward Her, light and obedient, a balloon in the night, ascending. Thank you, he forced himself to say. Thank you.

CELTIC STUDIES

WHETHER FROM BAD TIMING, bad luck, or bad judgment, Meg McCarty woke up the morning of her forty-sixth birthday convinced that the one thing she wanted was a husband. Her friends tried to talk her out of it. A group of handsome, active, independent women, most were divorced or content being single. Not Meg. She'd worked hard all her life. She'd put her three younger sisters through college, paid off her dead father's debts, and nursed her elderly mother until she in turn passed away. Now at last, Meg was free. She did not want a little dog. She did not want a gay friend. She did not want a sports car. She wanted a permanent man in her life.

"You'll never find one in San Francisco," her friends warned.

Meg suspected this was correct. She began to look at other cities, other states, other countries. One day at work she opened a blog on Ireland. It claimed that Irish men liked women. That was unusual enough to make Meg read on. It seemed that Irish men were devoted to their mothers, loyal to their sisters, proud of their daughters, and faithful to their wives. Rape statistics were low; spousal battery statistics were low. A shiver ran through her. She researched further. The men her age in Dublin were mostly married businessmen, the men her age in Cork were mostly married shop owners, but the men in Galway were mostly unmarried and many—Galway was a university town on the west coast—were scholars, poets, and artists.

"Romantics," Meg mused. She wrote the university and enrolled in a month-long summer course that included lectures on Irish poetry, archeology, and history, and—why not?—fairytales, all subjects she loved. She took a leave from her job at the ad agency, sublet her apartment, and said goodbye to her skeptical friends, most of whom, with straight faces, asked to be invited to the wedding. "You will be," Meg promised, and took off on Aer Lingus.

She had packed flimsy new underwear and sturdy new walking shoes but she did not realize she'd forgotten her umbrella until the plane landed in rain at Shannon Airport. That was all right; she would simply ask some unattached male to share an umbrella with her. She had always been shy but the time for shyness was past.

The first Irishman she met was the customs official. He had merry eyes, a tuft of sparse beard, and ringless fingers. "McCarty," he said, examining her passport. "Now tell me, love, how Irish are ye?"

"Both sides," Meg lied. She had dyed her hair red for this trip and bought green contact lenses which made her eyes water in a way she hoped was appealing. She brushed a tear aside and bit down so hard on her single dimple it hurt.

"And how many generations would that be?"

"How many generations what?"

"Since ye emigrated."

"Two?"

Wrong answer. The customs man tugged his tuft and waved her on. Dismissed, Meg dropped her passport back into her purse. On the way out she saw the little boy she'd held on her lap during most of the flight. He waved, shy and joyful. He had stayed awake all night with her, looking at the moon shining over the Atlantic.

"We're here," he whispered, as if sharing a secret. "In Ireland!"

"Yes!" She bent to give him the last roll of lifesavers in her coat pocket. "Ireland!"

As she straightened, she wondered what "Ireland" meant to him, a six-year-old kid traveling alone—a plate of cookies waiting on his grandparents' kitchen table? a fishing trip to Galway Bay? She scanned the crowd. He might have an interesting uncle—Ireland was full of bachelor uncles—but the boy was picked up, hugged, and carried off by two teenaged girls. Turning, she saw one of the flight attendants pass by, pulling his suitcase. He had a model's uninteresting beauty—even features, smooth tan, white teeth—and he nodded to her with a regal dip of his sleek head. She remembered how useless he'd been on the plane, spilling hot coffee on her as he chatted with another attendant, and how, twice, he'd forgotten to bring the boy's milk. She did not nod back.

Instead, she hefted her own suitcase with its brave festoon of green ribbon off the baggage carousel and reset her watch. The quiet throb in her left ovary made itself felt again, a small pain that had been sounding its warning the last few months. She waited for it to pass, then ran lip-gloss over her dry lips, rearranged her cleavage, and approached three men one at a time to ask directions for the Galway bus stop. The three could have been cousins. Neither handsome nor plain, they were uniformly pale, with a moist sheen to their beardless faces. They had light eyes, light hair. Their beauty lay in their voices, sweet and lilting, as each in turn pointed in a different direction and said, "You can't miss it."

Meg got the correct directions from a girl at the Information Desk and headed outside. The rain smelled fresh and she laughed to see two gulls wheeling white over the parking lots: a good sign, she decided.

The bald man waiting at the bus shelter was not exactly hostile when she asked (again) if this was the right stop for Galway; simply jabbing at the schedule right in front of her could be seen as helpful. She smiled once or twice to get his attention but he stared into the distance, smoking, and so she resorted to silence herself, which could be seen as mysterious. Rain flattened her hair and ran down the inside of her collar. The man preceded her onto the bus (the driver was a woman) and turned toward the window; she was about to sit next to him but that seat was claimed by an old lady who pulled out a rosary and began to kiss it with a furtive aggression that was too private to watch. Meg settled farther back, beside a freckled schoolgirl who held her cell phone as if it too was a holy object, looking down at it with lips moving in her own silent prayer, one Meg knew well, *Please let him call me Please let him call me.*

Meg turned her attention to the window. Green fields, brown cows, white daisies, low stone walls. Would her intended live on a farm? He'd be good with horses and give thrilling massages. Or maybe He'd live in a small town like the one the bus was passing through now, in one of those cottages with a yellow door and a yard overgrown with poppies. Or perhaps He was a wealthy physician, summering in that stone house, half hidden in woods. "How do you know 'He' even exists?" her friends had teased before she left and Meg had laughed with them because of course she didn't know. Ever since deciding to come, she'd been blessed with conviction and blinded to facts. All she knew was that she'd find Him here, somewhere, soon. She leaned back in her seat and woke up with a dry throat and drool on her chin when the bus stopped in Galway.

The cab driver, like the customs man, started off as flirtatious. "You're here for the university, are ye, love?" His voice was warm and tender, but he said nothing more after Meg volunteered that yes, she was taking a course called Celtic Studies. Was that the wrong thing to say? Was there a secret response she didn't know? These men! They threw the ball, she threw it back, they dropped it. The cab driver was good looking, about her age, pale, like all of them, and, like all of them, able to grant the first "love" and no other.

Of the town of Galway she saw little—a warren of gray streets around a torn up main square. Her room was at the edge of the city, by the river, in a student housing complex with a Gaelic name she could not pronounce. She had agreed to share with three other Americans, all of whom, she suspected, would be years younger than she, but that was all right, she liked young people, and besides, she wouldn't be home much. She planned to spend her free time in the pubs, reading poetry and prettily nursing a Guinness until He approached and sat down beside her.

A few hours later, after a nap and a shower, that was exactly where she found herself, but the seat across from her was occupied by one of her housemates, Lydia, a nineteen-year-old from Tucson with cerebral palsy. "I can't carry my own books," Lydia was explaining. "I need help going up and down stairs and getting on and off buses. I have no peripheral vision." She stopped to give Meg the same gentle but commanding look Meg had received the last few years from her invalid mother. "Also, I can't really cook for myself."

"That's all right," Meg heard herself saying. "I'll cook for you."

Lydia gave a lopsided smile and stood up. She wore thick glasses but she had pure pink and white skin, like a girl dipped in rose milk, and a plump mouth sudsy with white teeth. She had large breasts and as she lurched away they plunged inside her tee shirt like fat puppies on leashes. *She'll get laid before I do*, Meg thought. "Don't worry," Lydia said, as if she were reading her mind. "This is the safest pub in Galway. In terms of men, I mean. They don't hit on you here."

And they didn't. Meg finished her drink, trying, by osmosis, to attract the two men beside her who were in deep discussion and even deeper agreement, nodding and encouraging each other, but what she heard ("There was a man hung himself in those woods back of Conneely's." "Why?" "Who knows! There was a tree!") had to have been a joke, and though she laughed appreciatively, neither man did.

Embarrassed to be caught eavesdropping, she slipped off her stool and walked outside. It was nine at night, but still light, so she left the town behind and walked down the river path. Lupine, wild roses, yellow iris and buttercups grew along the bank and the evening air smelled of sweet clover. Rounding a bend, she saw a ruined castle across the river, its stone turrets green with ivy, swallows darting through its open windows. Two actual swans swam by. The setting could not have been more perfect, and when she heard footsteps behind her she turned, prepared, only to waste her smile of welcome on a heavyset woman walking two brown and white spaniels. A neon green tennis ball bounced out of one of the dogs' mouths, and Meg, after a sullen moment, scooped it up and threw it back.

Lydia, a bearded boy named Jeremy from Ohio, and an excitable Southern girl named Sheila were all watching television in the common room when she came back to the apartment. They had found a Gaelic channel—an interview with a retired hurling champion, a man of sixty with thinning hair, a scar on his cheek and an expression of such quiet sorrow that Meg stood on after the others went out to the pubs again, fascinated. So this was a true Irish hero: the thin lips, clear-cut eyes, grave voice saying, in the subtitles below, "The only thing I've ever loved in my whole life is this game."

Sad, Meg thought. She thought of all the things she'd loved, her parents, her sisters, her friends, her books, photographs, music, even her job. The only love she'd never known was the constant love of one good man and that would come. She turned the TV off and went into her room, with its built-in desk and study lamp. She crawled into her narrow nun's cot, pressed a hand against her throbbing ovary, and slept for eleven hours, dreaming unhappily of the flight attendant.

Classes began the next day and Lydia led the way, lurching toward the university so recklessly that Meg had to rein her back from the traffic at every corner, while Jeremy in turn stopped traffic as he took photographs to send home to his girlfriend, and Sheila, in a miniskirt, blew kisses to the furious drivers. Their professor met them at the door to their classroom and shook their hands as they entered. A few inches shorter than Meg, with a head of copper curls, a gold earring, and the broad chest of a weight lifter, Professor Riordan seemed unable to look anyone in the eye as he told them what

... he'd "like" them to read, what lectures he "hoped" they'd attend, what outings he "prayed" they'd enjoy. He twisted his wedding ring as he spoke, worrying it back and forth. Perhaps, Meg thought, he was abashed by the presence of the three pretty blondes from San Diego in the center row, or by Lydia's tight tee shirt, or Sheila's bare knees, or maybe even by her, in her itchy new Aran sweater and tam.

The afternoon session was taught by Dr. Shaughnessy, a thin man in a tweed suit who was supposed to talk about Irish history but instead spoke about the effects of fast food on the Irish diet and fast cars on the Irish roadways. For two hours he ranted against the speed economy that was killing language and literature, taking lives and ruining families. Meg liked his passion, and thanked him for the lecture after class but with a sly look past her he gathered his papers and darted away, as long-legged as a jackrabbit.

The next day's lecture was on literature: Professor Riordan, wringing his hands, quoted Yeats and Kavenaugh. Wednesday's lecture, taught by a limp young man in sunglasses, was on Celtic harp; Thursday's, taught by a married Chinese geologist, was on limestone, and Fridays, taught by a woman, was on film. The fairytale lectures had been cancelled.

It was clear that any fairytale Meg might have entertained about dating an academic was doomed, but Meg thought about Dr. Shaughnessy's rant as she walked toward the center of town on Saturday morning. Hadn't she come to Ireland to experience the very tempo he insisted was obsolete? To meet a slow man at a slow pace, with time to ramble and ruminate? Her life in the States had been so crowded with work and family responsibilities that she had not really had a chance to just . . . the word caught her up with pleasure . . . drift.

Drifting, she wove through the wet cobblestone streets fronted with sweater shops and craft shops and darkly recessed pubs, tipping the bad bagpipers and sloppy jugglers and quaking mimes, stepping aside for uniformed school girls and tattooed teenagers and couples pushing prams. Outside the shops, volunteers stood in the rain collecting money for children in Africa and Iraq and Afghanistan and almost everyone stopped to give. Music poured from the pubs—American music mostly, songs Meg knew, "Cripple Creek" and "Proud Mary"—the smell of fish and chips spiked the air, and the river flowed fresh through banks lined with wildflowers.

She walked through light rain all day and at seven thirty that evening found herself in front of the Town Hall Theater. She entered and bought a ticket for a play about a celibate farmer. It was a comedy and the audience laughed but Meg saw far too many parallels to her own situation. The poor farmer was loveless. He was crushed and eventually defeated by the church, by the greed and guile of his friends, and by his own timidity. Though she clapped with the others, Meg left depressed, remembering how the actor playing the farmer wiped the sweat off his forehead as he exited and his lost look as he bowed. There had been something about that actor she liked—the same quiet male dignity she had liked in the hurling champion—and she scanned the program for his name. Tim McCarty. Imagine! Her last name! They might be related! Though probably not. Her father's family had intermarried with Germans, French, English, Scotch and Native American—anyone who would have them—and her mother's family had been Jewish.

The rain was falling hard when she came out of the theater and she hurried to catch the shuttle bus. There was one other passenger getting on, an old man who sat down behind the driver. "What a night!" she exclaimed as she climbed aboard.

"Desperate," the two men agreed. They were already deep into a joke of some sort and lowered their voices to shut her out; the old man's voice, however, had a dramatic timbre that carried and so Meg heard about the Irishman who had sex twice, twenty years apart, but not, thank God, with the same woman. What was so funny about that? She shrugged as the two men burst into laughter and the old man got off and loped away in his jeans and denim jacket.

The next morning Meg awoke to a strange and welcome silence: the absence of rain. She dressed and headed out to the river path, again besotted with the romance of the yellow furled iris, the reeds along the riverbank, the pink morning glory threading through the sunlit underbrush. Her foot accidentally brushed a stand of dandelions, and she stopped, arms lifted, as the pewter fluff floated around her. What a magical country. Smiling, she crouched under a willow shrub and looked into the shallows, where, for the first time, she noticed a generic eddy of garbage, beer bottles, cigarette butts and condoms; her smile left and she was stabbed with sadness. She had no business being here. Her quest was naïve. She was no longer young, she was orphaned, childless, and had had her heart broken too many times in too many places to even count. She pressed her hand to a throbbing ovary and walked back to cook breakfast for her housemates, who had already started to call her Mom.

She spent the following weeks being Mom, helping Lydia up the narrow stairs of Blarney Castle and holding her as she bent backwards to kiss the sleek green slab before lying down to kiss it herself. She extricated Sheila from a club where she was being fondled by an exultant drunk who cried, "And wouldn't you be a nice girl to keep in a back room!" She gave her phone card to Jeremy who needed to call his girlfriend in the States and she walked each of the three blondes home after they'd thrown up in pubs. She applied herself to her studies and gave up looking for Him. *He,* she thought, *can look for me.* She read, walked, explored, took a ferry to the Aran Islands and a bus to Kylemore Abbey, moving invisibly but not unhappily through the crowds of other tourists, couples, and students. She climbed the Cliffs of Moher and Yeats' tower, traveled to Dublin to admire the Book of Kells, and twice returned to the Town Theater to see Tim McCarty. If she could not find a man to love, at least she had found a country. Every evening she walked by the river in the late summer twilight, something Professor Riordan told her was called, beautifully, "the simmer dim." The sky was always alive with drama, clouds piling and parting, and the peace of the place, the kindness and courtesy of the people, comforted her.

On the last day of class she was in the supermarket buying groceries for her housemates' farewell dinner when she saw a familiar face. It was the white-haired old man she'd seen on the bus, only he wasn't that old and the white was a bleach job.

"Tim McCarty," she said. "I've been in love with you for weeks."

He turned to her, wary. Up close, his eyes were startlingly blue. "It's a shame you're still celibate!" she said.

Her daring earned her the full weight of his attention.

Encouraged, Meg held out a carrot. "May I cook you dinner tonight before the show?"

The actor smiled again, pulled on a pair of expensive Italian sunglasses, reached out, took the carrot from Meg's hand, bit into it, handed it back, said, "No," and left.

Rude! Meg thought. The men she had met here were rude! Not kind, not courteous, rude! She wiped her eyes, which had filled with hurt, and dropped the carrot back into her shopping basket. I should count my blessings I never met Him here, she told herself. Ireland—it was raining again—was a dreary country full of dreary people. She ducked her head and hurried back through the downpour, hugging her groceries.

She was more upset than she meant to be and that night for the first time she got drunk. She went to one pub with her housemates, left them to go to another with a boy in a torn sweater, left him to go to another where she met the dour long-legged Professor Shaughnessy, whom she gaily addressed as Doctor Speed Freak, and with whom she shared her innermost thoughts about the Celtic Tiger (meow), the Celtic Theater (zzzz) and the Celtic Cuisine (crisps beat cabbage hands down—she said that four or five times while slapping her hands palm down on the table). When he excused himself and did not come back she accepted an offer to dance from a Yugoslavian waiter and sometime around three in the morning she ended up with the boy in the torn sweater again. They went into an alley, she lifted her skirt, he entered, she felt the first sweet shock of contact and then nothing except the bruise forming on her coccyx as it bumped against the brick wall and the pain in her ovary. "Mind yourself, now," the boy said as he zipped up. "Thank you," Meg said and went home.

There were hugs and promises from her housemates as they left the next day and A's and gratuitous "brilliants" on all her papers. At Shannon, Meg, red hair growing out, gray roots showing, green contacts stowed in their case and bifocals back in place over her bloodshot brown eyes, gave The Fates a final chance to take over, but no charming stranger approached her in any of the endless lines and her seatmates were nuns. She did notice the same sleek flight attendant going through his same self-satisfied paces and when he came around for drinks, bending over her in unconvincing solicitude, she kept her eyes on her magazine. Just before landing, she unbuckled her seatbelt to use the lavatory, but when she stood the pain in her ovary kicked in so powerfully it brought her to her knees in the aisle. The last thing she saw were the flight attendant's hands, small, white, and far better manicured than her own, stretched out to catch her.

One of his hands was in hers when she came to, and he stayed with her as the plane landed and she was whisked off for an emergency hysterectomy. His name was Frank Flanagan, he was Irish-American, he had been in the priesthood in his twenties, left it, married, his wife had run off with another woman, he was raising a teenage daughter alone, he had noticed Meg a month ago, the way she took care of that little boy, he had thought about her, how lovely she was, and all he could say was it must have been God's will that had finally brought them together. His breath was bad, his teeth were false, he had been in treatment for alcoholism six times and he talked constantly, smoothing his hair and glancing at himself in every reflective surface, but Meg felt the life in his soft polished hands and held on. She would say yes when he asked her to marry him. She would be happy. She would make him happy. And all of her friends would dance at their wedding.

MOSE IN THE MORNING

"Tick tock," Mose says. It's 4:00 a.m. He's wide awake and thinking about money. He owes the gas company, the phone company, his dentist, and his bankruptcy lawyer. His truck needs brakes, his boat trailer needs tires, he's out of propane. There's nothing in his freezer but six five-inch catfish and a gallon of chocolate ice cream. He may have to get a job. What kind of job? Mose stares at the ceiling and twirls a hair on his chest which he knows, without looking, is gray as opossum fur. Mose is old, too old for a job. At fifty-five, he's old enough to die. Which might not be bad. Dying might be the only way to make him finally, decently, understandably, unemployable.

In the meantime: The bills.

Mose crosses his arms behind his head and thinks. He's good at this. He has a high IQ. You need a high IQ to stay poor as long as he has.

He could be a fishing guide.

If he knew where the fish were. He hasn't caught a decent croppie or catfish all summer. Plus his boat. The busted starter. The leak.

He could sell venison. If it was deer hunting season. If he had a tree stand. If selling venison was legal and no one Mose knew would turn him in. Some of the people Mose knows might. Not everyone's a friend. He found that out when he tried to grow pot in the woods. There are other things in the woods. Morels. Ginseng. Squirrels are out. Squirrels are hard to shoot; they won't stand still. As for turkeys: turkeys are dangerous. They attack. He's not hunting turkeys.

That leaves carpentry.Carpentry pays twenty dollars an hour now. The last time Mose did carpentry it paid six dollars an hour. The last time he did carpentry he busted his back, his knees, his shoulders and both hands and ended up having to marry the lady whose house he was remodeling.

He's not doing carpentry.

Doctor Lawyer Indian Chief. Butcher Baker No Relief.

They are all jobs.

Mose has had jobs. Not for years, but he's had them. He's thrown newspapers and scrubbed swimming pools and climbed oil derricks and waited tables and posed for art students and given blood and driven cabs and crewed on freighters and topped trees. He even worked in an office once, wore a suit and tie, took business trips, carried a briefcase. It was hard to breathe. Then one day a friend phoned from the hospital. She had cancer; she was dying. "Mose," she said, "I've been thinking about you."

Thinking about him? With everything else she had to think about? He'd held his breath then; he holds it now.

"You shouldn't spend your life doing something you hate," she said. "You should be doing something you love."

So he quit. And spent the next two years playing the banjo. Which he loved. And still loves. And brings in about eighty dollars a year. Still, when he imagines having a guardian angel he thinks of her, Janice Cordobella, with her bald head and the diamond in her nose. His then-wife always thought he'd slept with her. But no. He'd slept with her sister. Janice was too good to sleep with; Janice saved his life.

Mose exhales, reaches for the paint-spattered transistor radio on the bare floor beside the mattress and turns it up to hear the end of his favorite talk show. When he fell asleep at midnight the theme was aliens mutilating cattle out in Wyoming, but now the theme is time travel and the question "What Is Time?" is being addressed by a guy calling in from death row. "Time is what you DO," the convict says. Mose thinks about this as the show signs off. Is it a joke? Convicts don't joke. Convicts don't phone from death row either. Unless—joke—they have cell phones.

Mose turns the radio off as the news comes on. Same old same old—war everywhere, all over the planet—Mose had enough of war in Vietnam, thank you. When he came back to the States all he saw was war, war in the streets, war in the houses of his friends and family. He had to move to the woods, live in the woods until he could breathe again. Whenever he thinks of Vietnam he has to move, he has to get some air, he has to take the covers off.

Throwing the covers off wakes the woman up. Mose had forgotten she was there. He has been accused of sleeping with every woman in town, which is not true but people have to talk about something, don't they? This woman—her name is Lisa Ryan—he never mixes up names—is a secretary at the elementary school where he plays folk songs for the kids on his banjo. He saw her at the movie rental place last week; she remembered him; big smile, pretty dimples, yes, she'd love to come over and see *Rambo* again. Nice woman. Kind. Sort of an irritating voice though.

"Sweetheart?" Too high, somehow. Too shrill.

She wraps her arms around his waist and cuddles close but Mose has to sit up, his hip hurts, his leg cramps, he can't breathe.

"Do you always wake up this early?" she asks.

"Only when I'm thinking."

"So tell me, sweetheart, what are you thinking about?"

He scratches the palm of his hand. "I'm trying to figure out how I've managed to fail so successfully all these years."

"Oh." She giggles. "You didn't fail me."

He pats her breast absently, moves his hand away. "I'm going to go to Paris, I think, and play banjo in the subway." His fingers flex. "Man."

She looks at him uncertainly. "Paris?"

Mose smiles, doesn't answer.

"Well." Lisa Ryan sits up, pulls on a tee shirt. "Do you want some coffee?"

"No. I'll make some after you leave."

"You're making me leave at five in the morning?"

"You have to get to school don't you?"

"Not until eight."

"I don't want you to get stuck in commuter traffic." He looks at her puzzled face. "You can have some coffee if you want," he adds kindly.

Lisa Ryan picks her jeans off the floor, pulls them on, and stomps toward the kitchen. He hears her sling the water into the pot and light the stove the way he taught her.

Mose, alone, starts to sing. "Tumdatumdatum." He strums an air banjo, fingers loose and limber, long toes tapping. For a second he's not sure what he's playing, then it comes to him: "Rockin' Chair." This surprises him and he stops playing. He thinks about the carved willow rocking chair still stored in his third wife's attic. His grandfather made it. He's been meaning to get it back. Maybe he'll sell it.

No.

It's a great chair.

Could probably get two hundred for it though.

"Two hundred?" he says out loud. He whistles. If it's worth that much, he better keep it.

He stands up, scratches, and turns on the television to check the weather channel, the only channel he gets. "Storm warning," he calls into the kitchen. "Wind gusts up to sixty miles an hour. No fishing today." Lisa Ryan brings him a cup of coffee with not enough sugar in it. Later, when she leaves, he will doctor his cup with the whiskey she brought over last night. He hopes she remembers to leave it.

"Do you want me to lend you some money?" she says.

He pretends not to hear her. "Did I tell you my roof leaks?"

"I can give you a loan until pay day."

"Oh man. Look at that." He stares at the weather map, green storm warnings surging across the state. He sits down on a stool and leans forward. Lisa Ryan frowns at him.

"Are you going to sit here naked and watch the weather channel all day?" Her voice rises. Off key.

Mose looks up, hurt. Lisa Ryan has no idea what he'll do all day. Maybe he'll read two or three newspapers, circle boat ads, truck ads, travel ads to Paris, maybe he'll even check the want ads, make a few phone calls. Maybe he'll read the email on his slow limping computer, see how his friend Benj is doing in Arizona, see if that girl he met in the bar ever answered, maybe he'll look at the dishes piled up on his counter and add new ones to them from his late morning feast of chocolate ice cream, maybe he'll climb up on the roof and fix the leak, the warm quick wind lifting what's left of his hair, or maybe he'll just leave the roof alone and let the rain leak down on the dishes—such a lucky leak, right over the sink—maybe he'll smoke a joint or two and practice "Rockin' Chair" until he gets it right. Maybe he'll break into his third wife's house, get his grandfather's chair out of the attic and grab the cougar skin rug she's kept too while he's at it, maybe he'll restring his fishing rod, walk to the post office, phone his daughter in Colorado, finish an article he started reading two days ago in *ESQUIRE* about businesses that secretly invest in psychedelics, maybe he'll rewatch *Rambo*, or take it back, and, around noon, maybe he'll fall into a deep sleep and Janice will come in a dream and tell him how he can make money without working.

Anything is possible.

"Well," Mose says, "You've got to run on, don't you? And I better get started on my day too. Time's a wastin'. No." He walks Lisa Ryan to the door and tips her face up to kiss her goodbye. "Time," he corrects himself, "is what you DO."

"Whatever," she complains and he watches her walk toward her car. The birds are starting to sing from the trees, there is a belt of apricot flame in the east under the dark clouds and he can already feel the wind start to rise and move free and easy against his bare skin. He takes a deep breath and spreads his arms wide. Another great day.

FENCED IN

RUE CORKER WAS A BOW-LEGGED REDHEAD with an outraged voice, a sour smile, and a flair for fatal diagnosis. She was known as Nurse Hearse on the cardiac unit in Little Rock where she and Patsy Evans both worked, and her clairvoyance carried over into other areas as well: she predicted colleagues' affairs and divorces with nerveless accuracy. She was, as Patsy's boyfriend Reeves put it, "no fun," and yet Patsy often ended up spending time with her, touched by the older woman's loneliness, and flattered, she had to admit it, by Rue's mysterious devotion to her.

"You're the only reason I even stay in this town," Rue said, settling beside Patsy in the hospital cafeteria one winter morning.

Patsy looked up from her coffee, alarmed.

"That's all right. I'm sure Reeves never makes you feel important. All I'm saying," Rue raised a bony hand as Patsy started to protest, "is that you're not full of yourself like every other fool on this floor. You're modest. So modest," she paused, squeezing some lemon into her tea, "that you didn't even brag about winning the scholarship to the surgery seminar at Stanford next week."

"How do you know I won the scholarship?" For some reason Patsy felt frightened. "I just found out from Dr. Hersey a few minutes ago."

Rue shrugged, then twisted toward a passing orderly. "Would you *watch* where you're going?" she hissed. "Do you think we're in a *skating rink*?

Nothing's a secret around here. Look." Rue pushed her cup back. "You're going to be gone eight weeks, right? And you'll need your car in California so you're probably driving, right? Well, I want to drive out west with you."

"That's impossible," Patsy said.

"Why? Is Reeves going?"

"No. Reeves can't leave his . . ."

". . . other girlfriends, ha ha?"

". . . his job. Anyway," Patsy finished, "I'm not even sure I'm taking the scholarship. I haven't decided."

Rue made a little spitting noise, and Patsy flushed. Of course she was taking the scholarship. It was the break she had been hoping for all year.

"You've decided," Rue drawled, and then, in the next breath, "Please."

It was such a surprising word, Patsy stared.

"Puh-leeze." Rue clasped her hands and lurched forward and for a horrifying second Patsy feared she was going to actually kneel on the cafeteria floor. Rue's pale face pointed up at her, green eyes wet with longing. "Please take me with you. I've never gone anywhere, I've never done anything, I can help with the driving, I'll pay for the gas, I won't be any trouble, I promise. Please? Please? Just say yes. Would it kill you to just say yes?"

"It would kill *me*." Reeves, who had never done anything he didn't want to do in his life, sat naked on the bed, strumming "Oh! Susanna" on his guitar as Patsy moped around the apartment, dropping photographs of him into her suitcase. "Three days in a car with a nut case? Why are you doing this to yourself? "

"She has a good heart," Patsy said, her voice uncertain. She sank onto the bed and pressed her face against Reeves's bare chest. "Don't forget me?"

"How could I?"

Patsy could think of a dozen answers to that, none of which she liked. Eight weeks was a long time. "I miss you already," she blurted, unconsoled by the easy "Miss you too, babe" floating back on four chords. She rose, blew him a goodbye kiss, and wheeled her suitcase out the door. The minute she got into the car, she slipped in the CD he had made for her last night. "This will make you smile on the road," he'd said. "I like to think of you smiling."

Two seconds into Tex Ritter playing "Jingle, Jangle, Jingle," she burst into tears, turned it off, took a deep breath, and turned it on again.

Rue's address was in The Heights, a surprise, because Patsy had understood that Rue lived with an ill, elderly, and penniless father. But Rue, struggling with luggage, stumbled out of a handsome brick house and across a cropped lawn to meet her. She shoved a suitcase, a duffle bag, and a cooler into the back seat of the Honda and climbed in beside Patsy. "I thought you might've changed your mind," she said. She was wearing a child's ski jacket over cotton pajamas and clutched an enormous pillow. Her short red hair stuck out in jagged points. "Did you hear the news? Blizzards in Oklahoma. Flash floods in Texas. A three-point-two *earthquake* in California. Plus six pile-ups on the interstate, an overpass down in Albuquerque, and you know what else? They haven't caught the freeway sniper yet."

"Which one?" Patsy teased.

"There's more than one?" Rue was silent for a moment, and then: "What is *wrong* with this country? Is everyone *crazy*? What are you *listening* to anyway? Is that *cowboy* music?" She sneezed. A big sneeze, rough and messy, followed by four more. "Don't worry," she said through the tissue she pulled out of her sleeve. "It's just an allergy. I have a lot of allergies. Oh-oh. See that white van? They say the sniper has a white van. Pass him! Fast!"

She ducked down in her seat as Patsy, childishly, slowed to keep pace with the van until it turned off the freeway.

They drove through rain for another half hour, Rue burrowing through various bags and purses and muttering to herself, Patsy concentrating on the road. She was waiting for the surge of release that meant she was on her way, going in the right direction, doing the right thing, but even after they passed the state line she felt weighted and dull. There was nothing to worry about. The patients she had left behind were in good hands. And Reeves was fine. He had said she should go, had said he would wait.

"I'd give him a week. Men like their women to stay in one place."

Patsy glanced over, startled. Rue was pulling out a sketchpad and some pastels and was beginning to draw things she saw out the window. Cows, Patsy saw. Red cows in a green pasture. Black birds massed above them. Or were those vultures?

"You know Dr. Kahf?" Rue said, sketching in a rainbow. "He left his wife. You know why? Gay. And Dr. Hersey? Filed for bankruptcy? Know why?

Gambling. Had to take all five kids out of private school last week. So he turns to D'Angelo in the elevator yesterday and asks does he want to go to the racetrack. The *racetrack*! I couldn't help it, I said, 'You need to have your head examined,' and they both turned and stared at me. I'll be lucky if I have a job when I get back. Of course I'm not coming back."

Patsy frowned. She liked Dr. Hersey. "What do you mean you're not coming back?"

Rue closed her sketchpad. "I e-mailed my notice last night and cc'd every one of those quacks and told them exactly what I think of them. They're lucky I'm not going to the newspapers with the things I've seen going on."

"You did what?"

"I knew I shouldn't have told you." Rue reached for her pillow, hugged it tight and closed her eyes. Her nose poked straight up, her lips turned straight down, and her freckles stood out like pepper on paper. After a while, dreamily, she said, "Where do you suppose he is right now?"

"The sniper?"

"Reeves."

"Reeves is where I left him, Rue. In bed."

"Alone? Hey! Why are we stopping?"

"Because you're getting out here."

"Don't be mad! Look! There's a gas station up ahead! Let me fill your tank. Please? Please, Patsy? Puh-leeze?"

Patsy pulled into the station, left Rue at the pump, and phoned Reeves. There was no answer, so she left a message on his cell and at the bar where he worked, saying he'd been right: Rue was running her nuts. She turned just in time to see Rue leap back from the car, gas spurting from the dropped hose.

It took forty-five minutes to get Rue washed off in the restroom; she had to change clothes, scrub down, rant against the hose, the pump, the cashier and the petroleum company. She insisted she was not topping off, that the hose had malfunctioned. In the end the clerk gave them a free tank. Patsy paced and brooded. They were already behind schedule and clearly would not, as she'd hoped, make New Mexico by dark. When Rue got back in the car she still stank of gas, still sneezed, and still, unbelievably, wanted to talk about Reeves.

"Did he at least give you a goodbye present?"

Patsy turned the CD up. Gene Autry sang "Don't Fence Me In."

"What's that? His theme song? Sorry! Can we stop to pee soon?"

"You just did."

"I can't help my bladder."

The rain was behind them and weak sunshine spilled over the Oklahoma hills. Patsy pulled into a rest stop and when she came out of the washroom herself she saw that Rue had claimed a table under a shade tree, spread a white cloth, opened the cooler and laid out spiced shrimp, potato salad, and pecan cookies. "Oh, no," Patsy said. "No, no, no."

"But you're starving." Rue smiled for the first time as she handed Patsy a plate and fork. "You don't even know how hungry you are." Her smile deepened. Dangerous dimples appeared on both sides of her mouth. Patsy poked at the plate and handed it back. Rue ate slowly, savoring each bite. "I love picnics," she said. "Don't you?"

They stopped before dark at a motel in Texas. Grassy plains stretched flat on either side and the air smelled as if there were a river close by, though Patsy could see none. The sky was a gorgeous mess of bruised colors behind the oil jacks and windmills. "Going to be cloudy tomorrow," Rue sniffed, as Patsy got out, registered, and paid. Patsy was beginning to recognize that it took Rue three times as long to get out of the car as it took her, and four times as long to get in it again. The car was already trashed with tissues, orange peels, and fast-food wrappers. Patsy claimed the bed closest to the door in the motel room, and stretched out. Arms around her pillow, Rue followed her into the room, sniffed again, and said, "Oh oh. Someone's been smoking in here; I can smell it. I'm going to go right back and get us another room."

Off she marched. But the next room had once harbored a cat. She could not sleep in a room full of dander. The room after that had a defective showerhead. The room after that was too close to the swimming pool. The room after that reeked of insecticide and the room after that—surprise—cost them nothing. The manager was worn out. Patsy was too. She left Rue taking a shower, and went out to find a cold six-pack and some peace. Still no answer at Reeves's. It was his night off. She tried to imagine where he could be—with a friend? What friend? A woman friend? Reeves's men friends were musicians like him, solitary men who stayed out all night. She drove around the empty Texas town with its wide streets, railroad yard, and deserted storefronts, humming tunelessly to the cowboy lyrics she was beginning to know by heart.

She came back to find Rue talking on her cell phone. She was naked, a small white curl of female flesh clutching a pillow. Her breasts, Patsy noticed, surprised, were bigger than her own. "No, sir," she was saying, "Yes, sir. No, sir. Yes."

"Who's 'sir'?" Patsy asked, when Rue hung up.

"My father. I need him to send me some money."

"I thought your father lived hand to mouth."

"He does. Sort of. Pa's an orthodontist."

"That's the first joke I've ever heard you make, Rue."

"It's not a joke." Rue giggled and leaned back on her pillow. "If he knew what I was doing right now."

"Doesn't he?"

"No. He thinks I'm just away for the weekend and then going right back."

"You are going right back."

"No, I'm not. I'm going to stay in California with you."

"What?"

"Please, Patsy?"

"You're flying home as soon as we get there, Rue. That's the deal."

Silence.

"You have a plane ticket."

Silence.

"You don't?"

Rue squirmed and mewed softly, "I want to see the Pacific Ocean. I want to see the Golden Gate Bridge. I won't be any trouble. I can stay in your dorm while you're in class and then on weekends we—"

"No."

Rue was silent. Exhausted, Patsy sank down on her bed. Rue had taken her pajamas out and laid them out on her pillow. Some wildflowers she'd picked earlier struggled to revive in a water glass on her nightstand. Pecan cookies were arranged prettily on a paper plate and one of Reeves's photographs, which Patsy had propped against the lamp, was tipped sideways. Patsy straightened it, went into the bathroom, changed, returned, and slipped under the covers. She closed her eyes, feeling the car still rushing underneath her, missing Reeves, the supple length of him, the warm silk of his skin. She'd been an idiot to leave him and she'd give anything to be back in his musty bed right now, listening to him pick out a new tune on his guitar.

In the middle of the night she thought she heard a voice, woke up, opened her eyes and stared at the motel ceiling as lights from the highway passed back and forth. When Rue whispered her name again, Patsy froze and closed her eyes.

The next morning, between sneeze attacks that twisted her whole body sideways, Rue offered to drive—an easy offer to refuse. By ten o'clock the clouds had lifted, the sun was pale but steady, and blackbirds were springing from the flat fields. Patsy listened to Bob Wills and Roy Rogers while Rue steadily slandered everyone in the hospital, from the head administrator to the janitor. When she had exhausted the staff, she lit into the architect who had designed the hospital, the town council that had approved it, and the public health policies in Washington, D.C. "Is everyone *insane*?" she asked. She stared out the window. "Where are all those cars *going*? What is that *mattress* doing by the side of the road? How do these people *live*?"

It was not until they stopped for lunch that Rue noticed something terrible: her pillow was gone.

It was a special pillow, it was the only pillow she was not allergic to, it cost a hundred dollars, could they go back to the motel and get it?

No.

Rue started to stab at her cell phone but it didn't work, then she borrowed Patsy's and it didn't work. Trembling, she sobbed between sneezes until they came to a gas station. Patsy gave her the number of their last motel, dumped all her change into her palm, and went to sit in the car. Rue was on the phone for forty-five minutes. Mexican field workers lined up, and gave up, behind her. Patsy tried to interrupt by tapping her shoulder, tapping her watch. Rue shook her away. She was having a problem with the maids, she explained. They were too stupid to understand English. Why did motels hire people from Calcutta who couldn't speak English? All they had to do was send the pillow C.O.D. to Pa's office. But oh, no, you'd think she'd asked for the moon. In the meantime, she did not know how she would sleep. She probably would not be able to sleep at all.

Patsy went back to the car and turned the key. Rue had credit cards; she could get to the coast on her own. She glanced at Rue's cooler and duffle bag and decided to leave them on the parking lot pavement, but as she reached across the seat, Rue appeared at the window.

"I love the way your hair curls," Rue said, slipping back inside the car. "Has Reeves ever told you how cute that is? Probably not. I doubt if Reeves has ever really looked at you. Or anyone else but himself, for that matter."

"All I can figure," Patsy said, her shoulders slumped as she started the car, "is that you slept with him and he dumped you and that's why you hate him now."

Rue laughed. "I don't hate Reeves. He's just not right for you." Before Patsy could stop her, Rue leaned over and fastened her seatbelt. "I mean, look at you. You're smart, you're lovely, everyone likes you, you won this great scholarship, you're going places, you have your whole life before you. You're a good person. And look at him."

Patsy did. With quiet pleasure she invoked Reeves's slim shoulders, dark eyes. She scarcely listened as Rue recited: "Pot every morning, whiskey every night, *smokes*—how could you be with someone who still *smokes*?—never married, goes through women like water, and how does he make a living? He bartends. Does he ever take you out, buy you flowers, give you compliments; does he even cook a meal for you? I don't get it. I just don't get it."

"There's nothing to get," Patsy said. "It's simple. We love each other." Patsy chose the word deliberately, hoping it would hurt. No one loved Rue. Patsy knew her heart's history: the fiancé who fled after the wedding invitations had been mailed, the thong underwear found in her last boyfriend's backpack, the married man who just wanted hand jobs. Rue hadn't had a lover in five years. Patsy had set her up once with an anesthesiologist at the hospital but after their one dinner together, Rue announced that he "wasn't interested in women," ignoring the fact that the very next day he started to date the blonde who had waited on them.

"Love," Rue scoffed. But it did shut her up.

By mid-afternoon, Patsy was caught in the weave of interstate traffic: pass, pause, pull out, pass again. She saw the windshield of the Accord, with their two small faces inside it, reflected on the mirrored back of one enormous truck after another. Blue mountains loomed ahead of them, looking impassable, and then were suddenly behind them, or off to one side as new ones rose up. Dead coyotes and rabbits littered the highway. The inside of the car smelled like bad breath and cough drops and gasoline and cold coffee, but the air outside smelled of sage, and Patsy opened the window to let it blow in, causing Rue to clap a hand to her nose while her discarded tissues lifted and fell. Rue was still sneezing as they pulled into the second motel just before dark and as the first symptoms of ache and fever began to clamp onto her own throat and temples, Patsy finally asked the question she should have asked from the start.

"It's not an allergy, is it?"

"I'm sorry! I thought if I told you I had the flu you wouldn't take me with you." And ten minutes later, more sorries, more tears. Rue had taken both their cell phones into the gas station to buy new batteries and now they were gone; someone had stolen them; nothing was safe. The evening was a flurry of intense whispered credit card calls to her father. Patsy looked up from the postcard she was writing to Reeves that so far said nothing but *HelpHelpHelp*. "None of it matters," she said.

Rue turned her face to the wall as if Patsy had insulted her, which she had, and lay without talking. But at 3:00 a.m. Rue said, clearly and quietly, as if continuing an ongoing conversation, "I lied earlier. You're not a good person. You're too ambitious to be a good person. You're cold and you're weak. You'll never be close to anyone. That's why you chose a man like Reeves in the first place. Someone no one could be close to."

"You're right," Patsy said. Her fever was raging. "You hit it on the nail, Rue. That's me to a tee."

"You don't have to be sarcastic," Rue said. "I'm just trying to help you."

The next morning Patsy's fever still burned and she felt achy, flaky, tired. "You'll have to drive," she said, handing Rue the keys. She slumped in the back seat and dozed. When she roused around noon she looked out at a landscape of beige plains and pink mountains and saw a highway sign that said *Grand Canyon 10 Miles*. "Whoa," she said. "Where are we?"

"I thought a little side trip would cheer you up," Rue said.

"Stop the car."

Patsy got back behind the wheel and didn't speak for the rest of the day. By nightfall they were in California. There was snow on the ground in Tehachapi but at the foot of the mountains there were palm trees, fruit trees, vineyards. "Can we stop?" Rue begged. "Just for a minute? Puh-leeze?" Bleary-eyed, Patsy shook her head and kept on driving, the highway a blur of black and white. She had to show up for her first class in two days and she was not going to miss it. At four that morning she pulled into a motel a few hours from the hospital and fell into an uneasy sleep like the day's drive on replay.

The next day she swallowed four aspirin and went alone to the motel diner. She read the newspaper as she sipped her orange juice—a quick scan and she saw that Rue could have written the entire issue herself. There was one article on the freeway sniper, another on the flu epidemic, and another on alcoholism and promiscuity in bartenders. She folded the pages and set them aside as Rue, rumpled and pale, slipped into the seat across from her.

"Salmonella city," Rue said, looking at the menu. "Look at the filth on this spoon. And what's that on the floor? Dried puke?" And, finally, "That guy in the corner? He's not a real cripple. Real cripples can't cross their feet like that."

Patsy looked up to see a fat man in a wheelchair reading the menu. "Real cripples can't drive white vans either." She gestured out the café windows at his car. Rue swiveled, looked, and turned back, her green eyes filling.

"I know you're mad at me," Rue said. "I can't stand it when people I care about get mad at me. I'm sorry." She clasped her hands together and bowed her head. "Just tell me what you want me to do. What do you want me to do?"

Be ready on time, Patsy wanted to say. *Don't forget your sketchpad, your cooler, your sunglasses, or your nasal spray. Don't be a bigot. Don't be a bully. Stop picking on Reeves. And don't be in love with me.* Instead, surprising herself, she said, "I want you to be happy."

Rue twitched and opened her mouth, but shut it again. "The phone in the room's free," she said meekly, "if you want to call him. I bet he misses you a lot." Which would have been fine if she hadn't added, "You're sort of his last chance, aren't you?"

"Isn't your father yours?"

Rue started to cry. The man in the wheelchair surveyed them calmly as he chewed on a toothpick. It was too much to hope that he might have a rifle. Patsy paid the waitress and went back to the room. Reeves answered on the sixth ring, relaxed and sleepy, and she laughed with relief. Here at last was the deep warm voice she had been craving. Yes, he missed her, yes, he'd been busy—played last night at a private party (*whose?*) wrote a new song called "Restless" (*what?*), cleaned out his hot tub (*why?*), was going to a gig out of town this weekend (*where?*), but would talk to her when he got back (*when?*). Only right now he had to run. His ride was waiting. Goodbye.

"Goodbye?" Patsy said. "I haven't even begun to tell you about the trip yet!"

But he had hung up.

She sat on the edge of the motel bed, holding the phone. The morning sunlight glared off the cheap mirror, the twin framed prints of the Sierras, the blind green expanse of the television screen. Rising, she saw the folder containing congratulations on her scholarship, her acceptance letter to the seminar, and a list of classes she'd be taking, one of them taught by a Nobel

Prize winner. She picked it up and pressed it to her chest, then she rolled her suitcase out to the car.

The man in the wheelchair smiled at her in the parking lot and she noticed for the first time the lettering on his van. *Tom's Tours and Taxi Service.* She turned and looked through the motel's diner window at Rue. From a distance, Rue looked small and lonely and harmless. But then Patsy saw what Rue was doing. Bent over the bill, she was re-adding it, stabbing an accusing fork at the waitress. "My friend," Patsy said to the man, "is looking for a ride. She wants to see the Pacific Ocean and the Golden Gate Bridge and then she wants to go to the airport. Can you take her?"

"Sure," said the man.

"That would be great. Oh, and one more thing. Do you like cowboy music?"

"Sure," said the man.

She gave him the CD and some money, helped him load Rue's luggage into the van, got into her Honda and drove away fast. She didn't slow to the speed limit until she hit the freeway again. The road stretched empty before her, the air smelled of ocean, the radio played Bach. For a long time she hunched over the steering wheel as if expecting a giant rope to whirl out of the sky and lasso her back in, but as the miles rolled on and she realized she was safe, she released her grip, unrolled her window, leaned out and whispered "Yippee," not even surprised by how sad her voice sounded.

ACCIDENT

On my way to the airport I hit a Christian. This was in Siloam Springs, Arkansas, on a hot afternoon last August, and it was entirely my fault: I wasn't looking. I'd stopped at a red light and had just punched the CD player off because Levon Helm was making me miss Jed and I was sick to death of missing Jed. When the light changed, I started up. The white pickup in front of me did not.

Cursing, I pulled over to the shoulder. As I reached into the glove compartment to get my insurance forms, I heard a rap on the window and saw a red-faced man glaring at me through the glass. When I opened the door, he leaned in, grasped my hand, hard, and dropped to his knees on the gravel.

"Let us pray," he said. It was not a request. He pressed my hand so firmly to his chest I could feel his heart thump against my palm. "Dear Lord," he began, "Guide thy errant daughter that she may receive the gift of the Holy Spirit and be washed in the blood of the lamb. In Jesus' name, Amen."

"Thank you," I said, pulling my hand back.

"Amen," he corrected. He glared at the tattoo on my ankle, two bluebirds that were supposed to be Jed and me forever. His eyes moved over the spill of cigarettes and make-up the impact had scattered across the front seat and, as I tried to tug my skirt down, lingered on an opened package of condoms lying on the floor.

"I'm awfully sorry," I said. "I hope you're not hurt."

The man closed his eyes and rose to his feet. He was about sixty, in work boots and overalls. He didn't look hurt. He looked strong and he looked furious.

"Get your cell phone, Sister."

"I don't have one. Don't you?"

His lips moved silently.

"I thought I was the only person in the world without a cell phone," I said.

"Get out."

Shakily, I got out and looked at his bumper. It wasn't bad. One small dent next to the fish decal. Then I looked at my VW. The license plate was smashed and the right headlight dangled like a plucked eye. "Jesus Christ," I whistled. I felt my hand grabbed again.

"Lord," I heard, a hiss of tight rage, "remind me that this blasphemer is Thy beloved child." When he opened his eyes to look directly at me, I was alarmed by their blueness. "Let's go," he said. And before I could even get my purse, he led me by the wrist down a gravel embankment into a strip mall. His walk was stiff and rapid. Helpless, I trotted beside him as we passed an IGA, a gun store, a pawnshop and a Dollar Tree. The asphalt around us sparkled in the sun and small American flags, strung at regular intervals along the shops, hung limp in the heat. We finally stopped at a low brick storefront at the end of the complex. A sign over the door said *Glorious Grace Fellowship.*

A large blonde sat at a reception counter under another sign that read *Rejoice.* She took one look at us and rose. "Pastor Mike!" she said. "What happened?"

"Accident," Pastor Mike said. He pointed at me.

"Do you want me to call the police?" the blonde said.

"Yes," Pastor Mike said. "I surely do."

The blonde picked up a white phone, dialed, and handed the phone to the Pastor.

"I'll let Miss Edna know you'll be late for supper," she said.

Supper? I looked at my watch. It was three o'clock in the afternoon. My best friend's plane was due to land in Tulsa at six. We were going to celebrate my break-up from Jed with tequila martinis and float the White River tomorrow. I hadn't been to the river since the time Jed and I had seen a baptism, a preacher dunking an entire family, mother, father, and seven skinny children, in the shallows. I'd wanted to stop the canoe and take pictures but Jed wouldn't let me. It's not done, he'd said. It's not done here.

Trying not to worry about what *was* done here when you broke the law, I picked up a magazine lying on a nearby table, glanced at the cover, which showed a baby wrapped in tissue with a gift card saying "From God" and was about to read a recipe for Coca-Cola cake when I felt a familiar grip on my wrist. "Sister?" Pastor Mike said. "Let's go."

I followed him back to the street. The police were already by our cars, a stout woman officer with a ponytail and a stout male officer with no hair at all. Their uniforms looked heavy in the heat. They knew Pastor Mike, he knew them, the blonde followed us out and they knew her too. The woman officer shook her head when she saw the front of my VW. "How'd it happen, hon?" she asked, the compassion in her voice making me tremble as I admitted, "I wasn't looking." I handed her my papers and she turned to the others.

"California," she announced.

"No wonder," Pastor Mike said.

All four turned to stare at me and I thought of California with a pang: its rundown freeways teeming with Atheists, Buddhists, Confucians, Druids, Gnostics, Hari Krishnas, Hindus, Jews, Muslims, Rastafarians, Scientologists, Shintos, Sikhs, Taoists, Wiccans. If I rear-ended anyone in California, I might be sued or shot but I would not be prayed upon. How had I ended up so far from home? It was because of Jed and his redneck charms of course, but why had I fallen for Jed in the first place, or, having fallen, followed him here, or, having followed him, stayed? Why had I thrown away my good iPhone just because his voice was on it? Why had I put his Levon Helm in the CD player instead of my own Otis Redding?

I blinked back tears as the police officers radioed their dispatcher. "Y'all all right?" a voice called from a passing truck, and as Pastor Mike waved, another car pulled onto the shoulder and dislodged three women who, hurrying forward to embrace her, could have been the large blonde's sisters. A car full of teenage boys pulled over to comment on Pastor Mike's bumper, and an old man struggling up the embankment from the strip mall took it upon himself to start fixing my headlight. An earnest little girl appeared out of nowhere with a box of powdered donuts which she passed around. No one was paying any attention to me. A butterfly hovered over the brown-eyed Susans blooming on the roadside; a mockingbird called from a flagpole; the air smelled of honeysuckle and fast food and diesel. I had almost forgotten why I was there and was startled when the police officers turned back to me.

"Next time, look where you're going," they said, returning my papers.

So I was not going to be cited? I hesitated, unsure, until the bald officer turned to a man in a Razorbacks tee shirt and asked about deer season and the female officer put her arm around the little girl with the donuts. Thrilled, I said, "Thank you!" and backed away to my car. Just before I turned the key I looked in the rearview mirror and saw Pastor Mike's blue eyes burning into mine; I hesitated, but when I lifted my hand to wave he also lifted his and then, to my amazement, spread two fingers into a Peace Sign. A genuine old-fashioned California Hippie Peace Sign! Grinning, I signed him back, started up, and turned west. I hoped my headlight wouldn't fall off before I got to the airport. For some reason I didn't think it would. For some reason I felt, I don't know, blessed.

GIVE ME THAT

BESS DIDN'T GO TO CHLOE'S MEMORIAL just for the cake. She had loved Chloe. Well, maybe not loved, Chloe was difficult to love, but Bess had admired her. Chloe had style. One week she would show up at their dream group in vintage Dior and the next meeting she'd be swathed in harem scarves and feathers. The men she sometimes brought with her were as striking as the outfits; Bess recalled a silent giant from the Balkans and a seventeen-year-old hustler who sucked his thumb. Before she'd settled down with Amir, a year ago, Chloe had been married four times, or maybe—no one in the dream group was sure—seven. She had acted off-Broadway, lived in an ashram, cooked in a famous New Orleans restaurant, studied painting with Jean Varda and was psychoanalyzed by Fritz Perls. Because she was older than the others—though no one knew how much older—and knew everything from Animism to Zen, she'd been their unofficial leader, the one they'd all turned to.

So there were many reasons to honor Chloe's passing, and the cake was the least of them. Still, the presence of the pink cardboard box on the passenger seat was a comfort to Bess as she drove across the bridge to San Francisco, and the smell that filled the car—a rich blend of chocolate, coffee, whipped cream and raspberry—was pure aromatherapy.

She steadied the box as she wound through the city, turned into the Haight, and began the long climb up the hill to Dahlia's house. She hoped there wouldn't be too many testimonials or too many tears before they ate.

The dream group could get soppy. With luck, Nicole had brought that good French cheese from Napa and Lisa had picked up Korean barbecue. Dahlia was doing the champagne, Zoe always brought pistachios, Ira had promised strawberries, and Amir, if he came, might bring a platter of Chloe's own couscous, which, Bess recalled, had big chunks of tender spiced lamb and plump Turkish apricots.

There might even be enough to take home.

It was not until she parked at the top of the hill and got out that she saw the full moon hanging over the bay. She paused, holding the box in her arms, and gazed up a moment, struck by something familiar in its round face, before hurrying on through Dahlia's gate.

The house hummed with low voices as she stepped inside. Four members of the dream group, all dressed in black, perched like crows on the white leather furniture scattered around Dahlia's living room—Lisa weeping prettily, consoled by Ira, Gina fingering one of her heavy necklaces, Nicole reading investment tips out loud from her dream journal. There was no sign of Zoe yet, but Zoe worked in Emergency and often came late. That eerie flute music Chloe liked played on the stereo, and one of the last paintings she had made—a portrait of a child asleep in a burning house—leaned against the glass coffee table.

Dahlia, also in black, met her in the kitchen. "A cake?" Dahlia said. "We've got so much food, Bess, why'd you have to bring a cake?"

"Chloe liked cake," Bess said.

"Chloe never had to diet like I do." Dahlia lifted the lid and looked inside. "God." Her voice was sad.

"Forty-five dollars," Bess said, and blushed. It was a stupid thing to say. Still, it had taken a huge chunk from her paycheck. "The house looks great," she added, glancing around at the flowers and candles Dahlia had set out.

"It should. I worked like a dog all day to get it ready. And now that every one's here, guess what, I want you all to go away so I can go upstairs, lock my door, go to bed, and cry."

"Cry?" Bess repeated.

"Sleep," Dahlia amended.

"It's like dying," Nicole said, coming into the kitchen. "You go along being brave and stoic and everyone thinks you're wonderful and then you break down and scream *Oh Shit* at the end."

They both looked at her, interested. "Is that what Chloe said?"

"It's what I'd say." They were quiet, for none of them knew what Chloe had said. Her last words to them had been "Don't forget me" and they had all meant to call but then Ira's computer had crashed and Lisa's husband had a relapse and Dahlia had her eyes done and Nicole's condo flooded and Zoe had that malpractice suit and one week had passed, and then another . . . Bess remembered Amir phoning from the hospital, babbling something that sounded like, "Get your drama club over here," but Amir's accent was so thick she couldn't be sure, and anyway she hadn't been able to get off work. She felt bad about not getting to the hospital in time, but what difference would it have made? Chloe had been in a coma. She winced as Nicole studied her skirt and sweater set, pink of all colors.

"I came straight from the office," she apologized. "I never learned to dress as well as Chloe."

"She always looked great, didn't she, even at the end."

"She really did. Terrific taste."

"Except for men."

"Amir. God. Does anyone even know where he came from?"

"Bangladesh?"

"And the one before?"

"Tasmania."

"And the one with the nose ring?"

"San Quentin."

"At least she *had* men."

The three were silent. Chloe had interpreted Dahlia's dream about a sink full of dirty dishes as a divorce dream, and Dahlia had since divorced, and she had interpreted Nicole's drowning dream as a fear of commitment dream, and Nicole had, in fact, broken off her engagement soon after. Bess, who sometimes made things up just to have something to say, had never offered a dream. She suspected Chloe might tell her she'd be single forever, a conviction she did not want confirmed.

"What did you bring for the altar?" Nicole asked.

"Just this. I've never used it." Bess, lying, pulled an old opium pipe out of her purse. "Look how it's carved. It has a little owl's head."

"Bird of death," Nicole nodded.

"No. Really? I thought it was the bird of wisdom," Bess said.

"Nope. Death."

"Oops. Well. I better go put it in."

"Take this too, will you," Dahlia said, thrusting the cake at her.

Bess carried the cake into the dining room and set it on the table—there wasn't *that* much food, at least not yet—picked up a carrot stick and a glass of white wine and examined the altar. Dahlia had covered a card table with red satin and on it propped the snapshots Chloe had brought to their last meeting, photos of Chloe as a child, wide-eyed, fluffy-haired, and for some reason stark raving naked. None of them had been brave enough to ask why Chloe had so many pictures of herself as a naked little girl sprawled on fur rugs and pillows, and Chloe had not explained. She'd been quiet that last evening, but seemed happy to be with them, curled up like a kitten in a cashmere shawl, smiling when smiled at but not speaking much. The only person she'd really talked to had been Zoe, and that had been about what kinds of pills to get in Mexico. The cancer, by then, had gone to her liver, and she never did get to Mexico.

"Did you see the full moon tonight?" Bess asked, as Lisa, wiping her eyes, came up to look at the photos with her.

"I know. It gave me the shivers. Look, do you think Chloe will like what I brought her?" Lisa pointed to a rhinestone tiara nestled among the roses and orchids strewn around the photographs.

"Perfect," Bess agreed. She looked at the other offerings on the altar. There was a scatter of maps representing some of the places where Chloe had traveled—Myanmar, Haiti, Easter Island, Transylvania. There was a candle holder with The Virgin of Guadalupe painted on it, a book of Rumi's love poems, a jade Buddha, a quilted Chanel backpack with a cigarette burn, a stained Hermes scarf, a pack of Egyptian Tarot cards, a can of black truffles, and a chipped crystal dragon. A disturbingly damp slice of *pâté de foie gras* gleamed on a white plate.

"Gina brought that. She's so dense sometimes," Lisa said, lowering her voice unnecessarily, Bess thought, for Gina was deaf and never wore her hearing aid. Lisa's eyes welled up and she started to cry again. "I know it's selfish but why did Chloe have to pass on just when I'm starting to dream about my stepfather again?" She picked up a photo of five-year-old Chloe on a garden swing, wearing a string of pop beads and nothing else. "It's not fair."

"I'm fine," Gina said, coming up beside them. "But I've never been so busy. The orders are pouring in." She leaned forward and studied the photo in Lisa's hands. "Pearls," she mused. "Maybe that's what I should do next." She touched the ornate stone necklace weighting her slender neck. "Parian marble," she said, when Lisa asked if she had gone to Chloe's funeral. "From Greece." She smiled and drifted off and Lisa started to cry again. Bess knew she was jealous; they all were. The idea to design jewelry had come to Gina in a dream that Chloe had worked for her. She had made almost two hundred thousand dollars off eBay this last year alone, which came, Bess thought, figuring quickly, to about four years of her own salary at the insurance office, though it probably didn't begin to match Zoe's income as a doctor, or Nicole's as a stockbroker, or Dahlia's as a decorator, or Ira's as an architect. Lisa was the only one in the group who didn't work, but Lisa was married to a developer and probably could have given Chloe a real tiara if she'd wanted. We all could have helped more, Bess thought, wondering again if Chloe had finally died, as Zoe had said, of starvation, and if it was also true that none of them had managed to get to her funeral. Carefully, she set the opium pipe down in the lap of a voodoo doll in a tiger skin bikini, then turned to Ira as he called her name and patted the space beside him on the couch.

"You'll never guess," he said and she smiled, prepared for a joke. Ira, plump and chatty, was her favorite person in the group, the only one to have a sense of humor. But the face he turned toward her tonight was blank with piety. "I met someone," he confided. "Just like Chloe predicted. Remember the dream I had about a white basin? Well, you won't believe it. Arthur used to be a priest! Now, of course, he works for Google, but isn't it just the most amazing thing? I feel I owe Chloe big thanks. She told me I wouldn't end up alone."

Bess thought again of Amir's phone call and was silent. Nicole sat down beside them. "You know what she told me? That a lover from my past would reappear, and lately I've been dreaming of my first boyfriend, but in my dreams his name is Scalpel not Samuel. What do you think that means? Should I ask Zoe?"

Dahlia came out of the kitchen. "You can ask her now. She's here."

Zoe always made an entrance. She had changed out of her hospital scrubs but still wore her do-rag and her glasses were smudged with specks of what had to be human matter. "Have we started yet?" She looked around, eyes bright. "Let's start!" It was clear she had decided to take over Chloe's role as leader; it was also clear, at least to Bess, that she lacked the gift for it; the group would probably have to disintegrate soon. "Tonight we'll celebrate Chloe's last dreams. I brought copies so everyone take one. Ira, you start.

Then around the room: Lisa, Bess, Nicole, etcetera. We won't work them tonight. We'll just listen."

Bess looked down at the paper in her lap. It was a short dream, featuring the same mother and the same seamstress that often cropped up in Chloe's dreams. Strange, that she knew Chloe's nocturnal life so well but had never had a Saturday bike ride with her, or a Sunday breakfast, or ever, even, seen her in the sunlight. The group had met at Chloe's apartment only once and she remembered it as big and bare, decorated with hairy brown masks from Africa and the Americas, and she remembered Chloe herself behaving oddly, telling them how every birthday her mother had made her re-enact her own birth—her mother would lie on a bed and groan and Chloe would have to crawl out from between her legs. Didn't Chloe say she'd done that until she was twelve? And there had been something about a one-eyed uncle and being smeared with honey and strapped to a picnic table to attract wasps? What a childhood! What a life! No one had known what to say! Had Amir been there that night? Bess remembered a slight, unsmiling presence in the doorway, black eyes in a young face, watching them.

She tried to listen as Ira, deep voiced, read a long dream about a car ride, which made them all jump because in the dream the car was a hearse and the license plate said GO4TH and Chloe had died on the fourth. Then Lisa read an even longer dream about taking a bath in broken glass and that made everyone shiver too. Bess cleared her throat for her turn. "I am a child," she read, "walking down a city street when my mother drops my hand and dashes into a dress shop. She has seen a wedding gown with a green sash and she says *I want that dress give it to me* and the seamstress is angry and says *No this is Chloe's dress you can't have it* but my mother snatches it up and says *Look how it becomes me* and then she disappears through a hole in the floor and I am all alone and I realize I will never have anything of my own ever."

Lisa started to cry again and both Ira and Dahlia said, "That makes me so sad!" Bess nodded. But she didn't feel sad. She felt repelled. Repelled and bored and hungry. Definitely hungry. She glanced toward the dining room table. Someone—Dahlia?—had taken the beautiful cake out of the box and set it on a silver stand. How it gleamed! A delicious mountain of glossy fudge, terraced with raspberries, ringed with roses.

She looked away and gazed around the room at her friends. There sat Gina, neck decked with rocks, and Dahlia looking as if she hadn't slept in days, and Zoe with her filthy glasses, and Nicole with her bad face lift, and

Lisa with her easy tears, and Ira with his polished nails. She remembered the first time she had come to this dream group, she had thought they were all crazy. She had listened to their confessions with amazement at first, and then with envy. For she herself remembered no dreams. There was a lack in her, an emptiness. Where others recalled signs and symbols, puns and portents, saw colors, experienced love affairs, were murdered by their parents or murdered their own children, had intriguing conversations, traveled to foreign places, breathed underwater, or flew, she had—nothing. She slept. She awoke. It had been that way all her life. The only way she knew she'd dreamed at all was the dull ache in her jaw the next morning, as if she'd been gnawing great chunks of empty air all night. The group had suggested hypnosis, meditation, chanting, journaling; Ira had insisted Bess drink a quart of water before retiring so she'd have to wake up mid-dream at midnight, Lisa had made her set her alarm, and Gina had even, once, phoned her at 3:00 a.m., repeating *Hello? Hello? Hello?*

Chloe alone had made no suggestions. Once when Bess, apologizing, had said, "I'm sorry, I don't know why I even come to this group. I bring you all so little," Chloe had turned to look at her. "That's not true," Chloe had said, in her sweet cold voice. "You bring your curiosity. Your loneliness. Your cynicism. And, of course," she paused, her large eyes glowing in that way that always made Bess uneasy, "your hunger." The reading ended. Dahlia passed around candles and they all stared into the flames, said a blessing for Chloe, and blew the flames out. "You know that dream Bess read?" Nicole asked, as Dahlia went around with a basket collecting the tapers. "It reminded me. Remember how Chloe would come up to you and look at your sweater or your scarf and say, *Give me that?* I gave her my new leather jacket, she wanted it so much. She wore it all through the meeting. Remember? And then she gave it back."

"Yeah!" Zoe said. "I gave her my diving watch. She kept it for an hour. I thought I was never going to see it again."

"I gave her my car," Ira admitted. "Two turns around the block before she came back."

"She never asked me," Bess said. Everyone turned to look at her. She shrugged. "I never had anything she wanted."

"Come on people." Dahlia clapped her hands. "Time to eat; let's get rid of this crap." Ira rose and waltzed toward the table, filling his plate with goat cheese, dolmas, olives, salads, strawberries, and breads; he did not take cake.

No one did. Nicole piled her plate with grapes, Lisa ate corn chips, Gina cut herself a slice of liver pâté off the altar. Bess sauntered into the dining room and, pretending disinterest, scanned the table for the cake's competitors. There were none. She picked up the silver knife, and, whistling a little, let it sink heavily through all six layers, pulled it out, richly grimed with gunk, lifted it and sank it again, easing a generous wedge onto her trembling plate. Still standing, she reached for a fork and was about to take a huge bite when the front door kicked open and Amir strode in. He was wearing one of Chloe's silk kimonos, loosely sashed over his bare chest. His eyes were dilated and he held a scimitar.

"Hi Amir," Ira said. "You're just in time."

"No more time." Amir's accent was for some reason remarkably easy to understand. "You've all had enough time. Line up." He waved the scimitar and held out a cotton pillowcase with the name of the hospital Chloe had died in stitched on the hem. "Rings, wallets, watches, cell phones, earrings," Amir said.

Everyone was silent for a minute and then Zoe laughed. "I get it!" she said. "What fun! It's just like Chloe to think of something like this. I bet she had it all written out before she left us." She laughed again and the others laughed too, stripping their wrists and throats and earlobes, tossing their wallets in without protest.

"Rings, wallets, watches, cell phones, earrings," Amir repeated. "Not that," he added, as Gina, watching to see what the others were doing, started to take off her marble necklace.

Bess, sullen, set the cake down, and began to unclasp her watch and unscrew her earrings. She was reluctant to throw her wallet in. "I need bridge fare," she lied.

"You'll get it right back," Lisa said.

"You think so?"

"Sure. That's the whole idea."

Bess dropped it in.

"She waited for you." Amir touched his chest with one clenched, darkly tattooed hand. A dozen of Chloe's silver bracelets clattered down his arm. His feet in blue running shoes poked beneath the kimono's hem. "And who came to say goodbye? Which one of you came to say goodbye?" His dark eyes moved from face to face. He spat. Then he left the house.

It took awhile. But finally it sank in.

"We've been robbed," Gina said.

As Zoe and Ira raced next door to use a neighbor's phone, Bess took the opportunity to retrieve her plate. She took it outside, found an iron chair on the patio, sat down, hunched over her lap, and dug in. Granted things did not taste the same in the dark. The cake was as gooey and sweet as she'd hoped it would be, but there was a definite chemical tang to the whipped cream and a waxy glaze to the frosting. The raspberries were mushy and the coffee liqueur had a sharp alcoholic bite. Still, she finished it. Sucking the fork, she looked up. There was the full moon again and now she saw its round face was Chloe's, piquant and secretive, huge shadowed eyes and mouth tucked to one side in a sour little smile. It seemed to say, *You got what you wanted, didn't you? And it wasn't any good, was it? And it's all there is, isn't it?*

Yes, Bess thought, and went back inside for seconds.

KANSAS

THE COUCH GLITTERS, the coffee table glitters, the rug glitters too. Julia pushes the vacuum cleaner around the living room, sucking up every speck of dime-store sparkle that the late afternoon sun points out to her. Fairy dust, Kari calls it, and Kari has been happily shaking it off her skin, hair, and clothes ever since she got the part of Glinda in the middle-school play. Now she pokes her head from the bathroom and trills, "The house doesn't have to look perfect, Mom! No one will notice!" She waves her curling iron in benediction, practices her tinkling laugh two more times, and ducks back to the mirror.

"Oh yes they will notice," Julia mutters. Tonight is the final performance of *The Wizard of Oz* and her brother Brian is coming to dinner with his two boys. Brian is the single most judgmental person Julia knows, fussy, picky, critical. Now that his wife is in the hospital again, he has become even worse. Hoping to take his mind off Steffie's cancer, for one night at least, Julia has also invited her new boyfriend Van to see the play. Her fantasy—charming people sitting around a table laden with delicious food engaged in pleasant conversation—is just that, a fantasy, and she knows it. Steffie has had a relapse, and Van and Brian won't like each other. Idiot, Julia scolds herself. What was I thinking?

She looks up from the vacuum as the front door bangs open and her handsome brother and his good-looking sons file in. A half-hour early! She opens her mouth to wail a protest but closes it instead and forces a smile. "Hello!" she says, "Welcome to my—"

"Humble abode," Brian finishes, looking around, and in his eyes Julia clearly sees the streaks in the windows, the sagging couch, the fireplace heaped with last winter's ashes. She is aware too of her tousled hair, tie-dyed apron, and bare feet. Brian and the boys are as always impeccable in pressed khakis, loafers, and polo shirts, but they look pale, unpetted somehow, as if all three have already been orphaned. Julia steps forward to give Brian a hug but Brian as always steps back. Not a family who touches, Julia reminds herself. Never was. Never will be. She turns to the children instead. "And how are you?"

"We bought a new car," eight-year-old Marty replies.

"An SUV," ten-year-old Matt corrects.

"Cadillac Escalade," Marty adds.

"Silver," Matt finishes.

"Wow," Julia says.

"Is that all you can say?" Brian asks. "Wow? Take a look."

Julia walks to the front door and squints out at the street. "It's . . ." She stops to search for the right word (*big?*) but Marty interrupts.

"Father!" Marty cries, "There's a cat out there! and it's about to jump on to the hood!"

"Oh, that's just Fidget," Julia begins.

"Get it off, son."

Marty moves purposefully toward the front door, Matt a half-step behind him.

"Fidget's fifteen-years-old," Julia calls as they stride down the path. She turns back to her brother. "She can't jump onto anything anymore." But Brian doesn't answer; he is still looking around the living room, one eyebrow raised. Why should she care what he thinks of her house! She knows it can't compare to his multi-room mansion by the golf course, but she's made a good home for herself and Kari and she's done it alone on her salary. She straightens her shoulders. "What can I get you to drink?" she asks.

"Fresh squeezed lemonade would be nice."

"I'm sure it would be."

Brian follows her into the kitchen and watches as she finds a generic can of orange juice in the freezer, mixes it with tap water, and pours it into the tumblers their parents used for highballs. She glances longingly at the cupboard where she keeps the gin but knows better than to offer it; Brian and

Steffie quit drinking two years ago when they converted to a fundamentalist sect that forbids alcohol.

"I wondered who got the crystal," Brian says, wiping a spot off his glass before he sips.

"You and Steffie got the silver."

"Yes, but we entertain. You don't."

"What do you call this?"

Brian doesn't answer. Julia can't read his expression; he looks both shut down and lit up. It takes a while for her to soften. The siege with Steffie's illness has taken its toll. For the first time she notices a streak of gray in her brother's thick hair.

"How are you holding up?" she asks.

"Me? I'm a basket case. Can't sleep, back's out, got this constant ringing in my ears. Ever going to get these cabinets remodeled?" He looks around with his brilliant somber eyes. "Can't you get your boyfriend to do it?"

"Van's a plumber, not a carpenter," Julia reminds him. "And I can't 'get' him to do anything." She looks down at the pot roast she's pulled out of the oven and begins to stab it a little too vigorously. "How is Steffie today?"

"Not good. Her temperature's spiked. They're going to pack her in ice tonight."

Julia turns with relief as Kari comes into the kitchen, trailed by her younger cousins. Kari has fluffed out her curls, put on rouge and lipstick, and is fully in character, wearing her Glinda look of benign surprise. She has to leave early and accepts the plate Julia serves her with a trill of thank you's before floating off to the table to eat alone. Julia hopes Brian will give Kari a compliment but all he says is, "What's this stuff all over you?"

"Glitter." Kari smiles at him. "Wait 'til you see the set, Uncle Brian. We used at least a hundred dollars worth of glitter."

"Wait until you hear Kari sing," Julia adds. Kari rolls her eyes and grins at her, slim-lipped. "She's the best singer in the show."

"No I'm not, Mom, you know I'm not. Calista is."

"Calista is good but you're better."

"Then who's best?" It's Julia's neighbor Lea Goldman, laughing loudly as she walks in. Lea never knocks, Julia reminds herself. She and her husband lived in Bali once, and in Bali, Lea told her, you can go into anyone's house at any time and use their bathroom or take a nap in their bed. "Look at those curls on you, girlfriend!"

Julia watches Brian's eyes drop to Lea's hips as she bends over right in front of him to examine Kari's ringlets. Once again, Lea seems dressed for the gym, in shiny tights and a cropped tank top. Her biceps gleam, her breasts bulge, her haunches are as firm as a little dog's. Is she showing off or is she simply unselfconscious? Julia can never tell. She makes the introductions quickly. Lea's face, as she straightens, is shiny, lined, and faintly bruised from her last bout of Botox and she and Brian shake hands without saying the words Julia is pretty sure both are thinking: *Republican?* from Lea, and *Goldman?* from Brian.

"You're in good shape," Brian says, deadpan.

"I used to be," Leah agrees. "But as I get closer to forty . . ." She waits, but Brian doesn't offer the expected protest, so she turns to his sons. "A few reps of kettleball these days," she tells them, "and I'm ready for the hospital."

"Our Mom is in the hospital," Marty says. "She's been there six times already."

"Seven," Matt says.

"Hey. Boys. Shhh," Brian says. "Why don't you stay for dinner?" he asks Lea who sits down promptly in front of the place Julia has already started to set for her. A car honks outside, and Kari throws Julia a quick kiss before she runs out the door to catch her ride to early rehearsal.

"Be sure and sit in the front row this time," Kari calls as she leaves.

"This time?" Brian says. "How many times have you gone?"

"Every night," Julia admits. "I'm a stage mom. Which reminds me—I bought Kari a dozen red roses. I better go get them. Be right back."

She has hidden the vase holding the roses in back of the coat closet. None of the buds have opened yet and she pinches one, worried. Bloom, she prompts it. She slips into her bedroom to change into a dress and sandals and pauses on her return to the dining room to look down at Matt, who is sitting quietly at the coffee table drawing on Kari's art paper as Marty watches.

"But these are terrific," she says, staring at his drawings. "May I show my friend Lea?"

Matt shrugs and Julia carries the pictures to the kitchen where Brian and Lea are sitting in silence. They all lean over Matt's work. He has sketched a battlefield of cartoon animals, wolves with ray guns and Uzis fighting monkeys armed with rocks and clubs. The drawing is energetic and imaginative and very advanced, Julia thinks, for a ten-year-old. It takes her awhile to see the turbans and beards on the wolves, the sunglasses and burkas on the monkeys.

Lea doesn't notice either, for she places the tip of one acrylic nail on a camel in a yarmulke, leans so far forward her breasts almost tumble out of her tank top, and says, as Matt blinks and steps back, "This is fabulous. You rock, kid. Ah," she adds, looking up, "The Van Man."

Julia straightens for a kiss as Van breezes in. His big shoulders, big smile, big booming voice always comfort and calm her. But tonight, even Van annoys her. He misses her lips and smacks her ear so soundly it rings. As she steps back she wonders what "The Van Man" means. Some sort of garbage collector? Julia met Van at Lea's house last summer, and she has always resented the Goldman's bafflement when they started to date. "Van's just someone," Lea always says, with amazement in her voice, "we met river rafting."

Lea sounds the same note of amazement as they sit down at the table and she looks at the dinner Julia has prepared. "Potatoes?" she says. "Gravy? And what's this? Red meat?"

"It's a Kansas theme," Julia explains. "It's what Auntie Em would serve." She adds a bowl of butter beans, a platter of corn on the cob, hot biscuits and a bowl of coleslaw to the table. "It seemed like a good idea," she adds, "at the time."

"So Lea," Brian begins. "Are you like my kid sister here? Or did you manage to actually keep your husband?"

"Of course I kept my husband," Lea says. She cuts a bean into three pieces. "My husband's in Montana this weekend. It's the opening of trout season."

"Fly-fisherman, huh. I'm a duck hunter myself. I tried fly-fishing once but it's too easy. It only takes, what, ten seconds to master that little hitch in the wrist? I mean, why bother? I like a challenge."

Lea laughs, but Julia hears the edge. "Fly-fishing's not a challenge? My husband would have a heart attack, wouldn't he, Van?"

"He'd freak," Van agrees, chewing.

"Thing about duck hunting, people think you're crazy out there at four in the morning hip high in cold water," Brian says, "but it's peaceful. No clients. No phones." He paused. "No bad news. Perfect."

"I suppose you're one of those people who take a dog?"

"Nah, I take Marty. I shoot a duck, I'll say, 'Son, fetch,' and he'll do it, even wring its neck if it's not dead yet, no problem."

"You're kidding, right?"

"I never kid," Brian says. "How about you, Van? You a sportsman?"

Van laughs and helps himself to another biscuit. "The only thing I've been killing lately," he says, "is time."

"Slow go in the sewage business?"

"It may be crap to you," Van recites, "but it's my bread and butter."

Julia sighs and looks down the length of the table. Her nephews are silently jabbing each other with their silverware and Brian is smirking down Lea's cleavage and Van is salting and resalting his plate and none of them are talking.

"Someday I'll wish upon a star," she starts to hum, "and wake up where the clouds are far . . ."

"Please," Brian says. "Not while we're eating."

"How do you stand him?" Lea says later in the car. "If I had a brother like that, I'd kill him."

"He's under a lot of stress . . ." Julia doesn't finish. Why defend Brian? He's never defended her. Yes, his wife is sick, but he has a housekeeper, a nanny, a gardener and the support of the entire Christian Right to help him. He does not have to do everything alone the way I do, Julia thinks. And Lea! Lea, too, has an easy life, with her wealthy husband who is never home. She frowns as Lea props her feet on the dashboard. Lea does not have to be at work at a job she hates Monday morning at seven, does not have to worry about raising a growing daughter alone, does not date a man who makes jokes about crap. She slams her old Mazda into the school parking lot and parks beside Brian's SUV.

"Here," Lea says, leaning forward. "Give me the keys. I'll key it."

"Are you kidding?"

"I don't kid." Lea's imitation of Brian makes Julia laugh. But she holds on tight to her keys.

The school auditorium is jammed. "You really live in Handy Man Land out here, don't you," Brian says as he settles his children into the folding chairs of the closest row they could find. "I've never seen so many pickup trucks in one parking lot in my life."

"You ought to get out more," Julia says. "Living in a gated community can warp your world view. Can you see?" she adds to Marty. "Want to sit on my lap?" He shakes his head. No. Of course not. He's too big. Matt is too big too. They sit stolidly staring at the backs of the adults seated in front of them. Julia turns to Van and takes his hand. She loves his hand, warm and rough and strong. He gives it a quick squeeze and then says, his voice against her ear, "Thinking of joining Lea's gym?"

Julia laughs. "No! Why? Do you think I need to?"

Van doesn't answer.

"Well hell," Julia says. She retracts her hand and turns away to watch the show.

The Wizard of Oz, when you've seen it three times, goes quickly, but Julia finds herself shocked, tonight, by all the references to death. She has never noticed them before. When the Munchkin coroner comes to examine the witch under Dorothy's house, Julia finds she is holding her breath. There is nothing funny about a coroner. There is nothing funny about "Ding Dong the Witch Is Dead." She glances at her nephews. Their faces are pale and expressionless. Why did she think this terrible play could take their minds off Steffie? She frowns and turns back to the stage. Maybe Kari's performance can lighten things up.

Kari's solo is the highlight of the show. She looks like a little wedding cake, her tinkle is tone-true, her smile is dippy as a stoned debutante's, and her soprano is so pure that Julia's heart floods. Julia scans the applauding audience for Kari's father and his fiancée but they haven't shown up since opening night. Good, she thinks. Let them miss this pleasure. Smiling, she turns to Brian, and is shocked to see him sitting with his eyes closed. Matt is looking down at a tiny iPad in his lap. Marty is asleep.

At intermission, Brian tells Van and Lea about a variety show his church put on. "We had professional lighting," he says. "Plus professional sets and costumes of course. But this production tonight I will say has . . . character. Especially that little chica Calista. We had a Mexican kid just like her in our choir."

"That right?" Van dunks his second brownie from the PTA booth into his paper cup of coffee and dabs at his mustache. Lea is stretching—or whatever you call it—sticking her butt in the air. These people! Julia turns away, savagely irritated. If only she could trade the entire lot in right this moment and be given a brainy Scarecrow, a brawny Lion, a sentimental Tin Woodman in return—how easy it would be to love those imaginary characters, and how hard it is to even tolerate the real friends and family surrounding her. She pats the bouquet of tight red roses in her lap. *Birds fly over the rainbow,* she thinks, *why then, oh why can't I?*

She is glad when the lights go down and she can watch Kari again. But Calista, as Dorothy, gets a standing ovation on her next song and Kari does not take it well. She stands outside the spotlight with sadness visibly pitting her face: poor Kari! Everyone gets jealous, Julia thinks. All my life I was jealous of Brian and for what? I wouldn't want to be him now. I wouldn't want to be Lea with all her money and leisure either. At the curtain call she hurries to the front of the stage and hands Kari the roses. "You were perfect," Julia tells her. "Absolutely perfect."

"Did Uncle Brian think so?"

"Yes! He'll tell you himself in a minute."

But Brian has gathered his boys and is ready to leave. "That was about two acts too long for us," he says. "I've got to get these campers back to civilization."

Julia waits for him to say Thank you for dinner or Enjoyed the show but he says nothing else so she says, "Okay then. I'll call the hospital tonight about Steffie."

"Sure thing."

The boys stiffen as she leans down to kiss them goodbye. Don't worry, Julia wants to assure them. No matter what happens to your mother, your father will never let you come live with me. She watches them march toward their car. Then she turns to Lea, who is also ready to go. "I have yoga first thing tomorrow," Lea reminds her.

"I promised to help with clean-up," Julia says. "It will be a few minutes before I can take you home; it will go a lot faster if you help."

"I don't do clean-up."

Julia smiles but it isn't a joke; Lea bends down, touches her toes, and stays there, counting to herself.

The auditorium floor is sticky with spilled drinks, crushed brownies, wadded napkins, paper cups. Julia moves down one aisle after another filling a garbage bag. She sees Van across the room; he too has taken a garbage bag but he is helping someone else, a young woman in tight jeans—Calista's mother. His big laugh booms back at her and she realizes it sounds even louder than usual because everyone else is crying. Munchkins are sobbing in each other's arms, the Tin Woodman is being consoled by the Wicked Witch, the Scarecrow is prostrate, surrounded by hiccupping Poppies. "Oh Mom!"

Kari calls. She runs toward Julia and presses her wet flushed face against Julia's chest. "This is the happiest I've ever been. And it's *over*!"

Not a minute too soon, Julia thinks, when she's home later that night. She looks at the uncleared dining room table, the dishes stacked in the kitchen sink, and realizes she hates everybody—Van for not coming back to the house with her, Lea for showing Van her "secret" tattoo in the parking lot, Brian for being Brian. The only people she's not angry at are the children and Steffie. Thinking of Steffie she goes to the phone and dials the hospital. She's put on hold a long time before the nurse answers. The news, the nurse says, is good. Steffie's temperature is down to normal. "In fact, she's awake right now," the nurse says. "Would you like to talk to her?"

"Hi, Julia." Steffie's sweet voice. "How did it go tonight?"

"Perfect."

"You and Brian. Always using that word." Julia hears the familiar shuffle of pages—Steffie looking through her Bible for an appropriate quote. "*Let us fix our eyes on Jesus*," Steffie begins, but Julia has stopped listening. There's no doubt about it: she feels hurt. No one has ever compared her to Brian before. The final insult of the evening, and it had to come from the nicest person. Sodden with self-pity, she says good night to her sister-in-law and retrieves the bouquet Kari dropped on the coffee table; the stems are battered and bent and the buds are already so greased with glitter they look plastic. Will they even be able to open? Do they even smell? She bends to get a whiff of their scent. Nothing.

She jams the roses into an old jar filled with water, sets the jar on the mantel, flops down on the couch and kicks her shoes off. The house settles close and dull around her. She might as well be in Kansas, the night is that humid, the brown air that flat. The room still stinks of the failed dinner and Brian's expensive cologne. The sounds of the night—a cricket call, the flap of moths against the glass, Fidget's uneven limp as he crosses the carpet—are too familiar to be forgiven. What is this crap about no place like home? Home is where you hang your head, home is where they have to let you in, home is what you make it. And what, she thinks, have I made it?

Impatient, she swings her bare feet off the couch and stands up. Matt's savage little drawings have spilled to the floor and she bends to pick them up. As she straightens, headlights from a passing car suddenly flare into the room, turning it into a dust storm of loose glitter. Caught in the whirl, she looks up to see the roses on the mantle spark into technicolor spangles of emerald and ruby, silver and gold. She stands still, enchanted. It can't last—she knows that—but for a second everything is just the way it's supposed to be: perfect.

BANYAN

JANE FLEXED HER NECK, rotated her shoulders, and looked up from her guidebook as the plane dropped through the clouds to the Big Island. She could see Mac and Mia, four rows ahead of her, Mia's tousled head turned toward the window, Mac's long legs stretched out on the aisle, both still asleep. How did they do it? Jane could never sleep when she traveled, too much to take in, too much to think about, but her lover and her daughter had crossed their arms and closed their eyes the minute the plane left Seattle five hours ago. They were going to miss their first glimpse of the volcano! She pried a macadamia nut from its package, aimed at Mac's neck and watched him start, rub the spot where it hit, then lean over and touch Mia's face to wake her for landing.

The old lady beside Jane snorted and Jane waited, expecting the snort to turn into one of the nasty low laughs she had been subjected to throughout the trip, but her seatmate only pointed to the open guidebook. "Romantic Hawaii!" the chapter heading gushed, "The perfect place for your dream wedding!"

Jane, shamed, snapped the book shut. She did not want her fantasies, mundane as they were (Mac proposing to her over mai tais, Mia radiant with approval) mocked, especially by this crazy witch. She was used to lunatics seeking her out and sitting beside her—she had some sort of unholy radar that pulled them right in—and this creature, decked out in stained sweats and hiking boots, carrying an ancient Shih Tzu in a bamboo cricket cage, had focused on her at once, settling down with a rush of incoherent mutterings. Her long white hair had a burnt electric stench and the long nails on her wrinkled brown hands were filthy. She had refused to move when Jane needed the restroom, and when Jane, forced to step over her, had tripped, she had chuckled. During Jane's absence, she had drained Jane's gin and tonic. Her dog, a horror of bristles, whiskers, snot and drool, had growled at Jane the entire trip and now, as the plane taxied into the Kona airport, began to snap toothlessly at her from its cage. Jane let her own lip curl back, then rose with relief as the seatbelt lights went off. She gathered her things and made her way down the aisle.

Mac and Mia were already out the exit door and Mia, on the tarmac, was already bent over, clutching her midriff while Mac, helpless, patted her back with his big hand. Jane quickened her steps to catch up to them.

"The wounded bird act," Jane explained.

Mia moaned musically, almost, if you weren't used to it, Jane thought, convincingly.

"She always does this," Jane explained, looking into Mac's worried face. "She's thirteen-years-old and this is how she travels. What is it, honey?" she asked Mia.

"I have a temperature," Mia said.

Jane pressed a hand to Mia's forehead. It was damp, fresh, cool as a petal. She bent and kissed it, feeling Mia's startled retreat. "You're fine." She looked up to see Mia's pretty pout reflected in Mac's new aviator sunglasses—huge, expensive, ridiculous glasses—why on earth had he bought them? At forty-five, Mac was still a good-looking man, tall and broad shouldered. There had been no need for him to dye his hair, bleach his teeth, and yellow his skin with self-tanner for this trip. He looked like a gigolo. Of course there had been no need for her to get Botox injections, scarlet lip gloss, and a new haircut either. No wonder Mia feels sick, Jane thought; she probably doesn't want to be seen in public with either one of us.

"Are you sure she doesn't need a doctor?" Mac asked.

"Positive. Smell the air!" Jane added brightly. "All I could smell on the plane was dog farts and old lady. But Hawaii smells like flowers."

It did. Flowers and coconut oil, ripe fruit and salt air. Alone at the carousel, Jane reclaimed their luggage, raised her head, and smiled up at a misty rainbow over the airport. She watched Mac drift over to a lei stand, choose a spray of plumeria, and drape it over Mia's bent neck. It was just like Mac, a landscape architect, to go to the flowers first, she smiled, and then winced as Mia, consistently bad mannered, hunched her shoulders, hugged her elbows, stared at the ground, and sneezed. It seemed Mia had given up on Lyme disease, mono, multiple sclerosis and leprosy for this trip at least, and had settled on a simple cold. Good, Jane thought. She could deal with a cold.

"You said it would be hot here," Mia complained. "I'm freezing!"

"I'm on fire," Jane countered. And her face, glimpsed in the window of the rental car as she slid inside, did look flushed and puffy, her hair spiked in damp strands, her nose shiny. An unwelcome shaft of heat shot through her as she slammed the door shut and tugged wrinkled silk off her sweaty chest and thighs.

"You all right, sweetie?" Mac, turning to back the car out, patted Mia's knee. "You need an aspirin or anything?"

"I can't take aspirin." Mia moved her knee aside and opened another of the enormous vampire novels she had been reading all summer.

"She chokes—Oh look!" Jane pointed to a second rainbow arcing across the sky.

The ocean glistened gray on one side and jagged mountains rose green on the other. The island was less lush than the guidebook had promised and had an arid clarity she had not expected. As they pulled onto the highway she saw the old woman with the dog. She was wearing a sequined visor and sunglasses and her long brown thumb was crooked out to hitchhike.

"Don't stop!" Jane warned, but Mac was hitting the radio buttons to find a station Mia liked and didn't even look up. Jane slid down in her seat as they passed. When she raised up, the woman was far behind and the road had opened onto a moonscape of lava rocks with messages and hearts outlined on them in white coral. *U N I 4-EVAH,* Jane read aloud. She reached over to press Mac's hand. He pressed back and she relaxed. Things had been strained lately, with her heavy caseload at the law firm and his recent lay-off, but they would be lovers again, she knew, once they were alone.

But they were not to be alone. When they got to Kona, they found there had been a mix-up and only one room was reserved for them. A holistic health conference had taken over the entire hotel and this was the last room available, the manager told them. "We'll go to another hotel," Jane decided.

"I can't afford another hotel," Mac reminded her. Jane dropped her eyes. The flight, the food, the rental car were all her treat. She had wanted to pay for their lodging too—the trip had been her idea and she made more money than Mac—but Mac had insisted. It was, he had said, the least he could do. It was also, Jane knew, all he could do.

"The room is big." The manager, a large, honey-colored Hawaiian woman, stretched her arms wide. "You'll like it. Two beds. Family style."

"No family I ever—" Jane began, but Mac took the keys and Jane and Mia followed him up the elevator to an airy room overlooking the roofs of other hotels and the ocean beyond. The two queen-sized beds were within hand-holding distance and as Jane shook her head, Mia, sneezing dryly, threw her things down on one of them, rummaged through her duffel bag, and locked herself in the bathroom.

"It's fine," Mac said. "We'll take it."

"But we won't be able to make love!" Jane could not keep the disappointment out of her voice.

"We'll just have to be inventive. Mia will be down at the pool, won't she, or out at the beach? Every teenage boy on the island will be offering to teach her to surf."

"Mia won't surf."

"You'd be surprised what she might do once she gets the chance. I might even teach her myself," Mac said.

"I thought you were going to teach me."

"You too, if you want."

He turned on the huge television, preset to a video about the island's volcano. "Kilauea's still erupting," he whistled. "Look at that." His bleached teeth shone unevenly below his dyed mustache as he whistled again, and Jane, following his gaze, saw Mia emerge from the bathroom in her new bikini. "You look dangerous, sweetie," Mac said, and Mia, with a filthy look toward Jane, sneezed again.

"You going to join us, Mom? We'll be down at the pool." Mac held his arm out to Mia, who stepped forward lightly.

"No. 'Mom' is going to stay here by herself," Jane snapped, "and watch TV all afternoon."

No one heard her. Mac's pleased voice faded as he led Mia down the hall. Alone in the hotel room, Jane opened her suitcase and threw her new lace lingerie into the back of a drawer. She reached to turn the television off, but the image of Kilauea caught her. It looked exactly like a black heart with red blood pouring out. She picked up Mia's discarded lei, sniffed it—why hadn't Mac bought her one too?—dropped it, and began to pace, her own heart beating faster and faster. She knew why Mac hadn't bought her a lei, hadn't sat with her on the plane, hadn't noticed her new haircut. In the last few weeks, Mac had changed. He had changed toward her and he had changed toward Mia. He had always treated Mia with amused indifference—his girlfriend's spoiled kid—but recently he had offered to help Mia with homework, had picked her up from dance class, taken her side in disputes over dishes and laundry. He had remembered her birthday with a pair of tickets to a rock concert, seemed almost comically disappointed when she invited a friend and not him, and had forgotten Jane's birthday altogether. His cheerful bedtime complaints about his bad back, bad knees, and leg cramps had sanitized their sex life and he had been "too tired" to even celebrate their two year anniversary last month.

A familiar yip sounded from the hotel corridor and Jane froze as the Shih Tzu shot past the open door. Was that evil hag following her? Wasn't this supposed to be the "big" island? She slammed the door shut with the flat of her hand, leaned against it, then sank to the floor, pressing her face to her knees. She'd read *Lolita.* She'd seen both versions of the movie. As an attorney, she'd defended child victims and she'd prosecuted child molesters. Nothing like that was going to happen here. She would just have to be careful. Very very careful. She put on her own bikini, turned off the television, and joined the others at the pool.

They went swimming, sunbathed, walked along the sea wall. As night fell, they sat on a green bench near an enormous banyan tree, watching Japanese tourists take pictures of themselves and listening to the clamor of the nesting birds above. "This tree," Jane remembered from her guidebook, "came from India hundreds of years ago. They call it the strangle tree because it can't stop growing. It sends out so many roots it ends up strangling itself."

"Dark and shady back in there," Mac said. "Looks like a good place to hide from the island police and smoke a little *pahalo.*"

Jane stared at him. Had he lost his mind? *Pahalo*? Mac never smoked marijuana, and he loved trees. The first time she had seen him he had been arguing with construction workers who were planning to take down an old oak outside her law office. But now he only smiled at Mia, tugged his dyed mustache, and didn't give the huge tree another glance. Mia, leaning against Jane's shoulder, sniffled piteously, swung her slim legs and didn't look either.

When the streetlights came on, they continued to stroll, cruising the art galleries with their airbrushed blue whales and smiley dolphins, the gift shops with their koa wood bowls and plastic grass skirts. They ended up in a New Age crystal shop. While Mia examined the soaps and lotions and Mac fooled with a "native" drum, Jane studied her charges. Mac was trying to show Mia how fast he could drum. Mia's indifference was heart's ease to observe, but that was because Mac was too new at this to know how to seduce her; you don't rope children in with things that interest *you*, Jane thought, you go after children with things that interest *them*. She watched his sad blink as Mia moved away. It would do no good to accuse him of being in love with her daughter; he'd be shocked; he'd deny it; he'd say she was crazy. And Mia would be equally horrified. Mac, she'd protest, was old enough to be her father, the father she hadn't seen since she was six, the father who never wrote or sent gifts—why would she want someone like him?

Someone snickered behind her and Jane swung around to see an old woman pass through the doorway. Setting down the tray of dyed shells from the Philippines she'd been sifting through, she watched until the woman disappeared in the crowd.

That night Jane lay awake listening to the surf, the trade winds, the call of the doves. Lonesome, she rolled over to kiss Mac, but he inched away, his body cool beneath the sheets. After an hour, she slipped out of bed, went to the desk, turned on a small light, and finished reading the guidebook. She had already learned the history of the islands—all that trickery, cruelty and corruption—so tonight she read the legends. She read about the miniature Menehune and their fish ponds, and about Maui, the boy who caught the sun with a fishhook. Finally she read about Pele, goddess of the volcano. Whenever anything annoyed her, Pele blew up. She didn't listen to excuses, apologies, or promises; she never held a trial, prosecuted a criminal or defended a victim; she simply erupted, efficient and brutal, and lava'ed everyone to death. You had to respect a temper like that, Jane decided, closing the book. Pele might have ended up alone, but she ended up satisfied.

She looked over at the two sleepers. Mac's arm was stretched toward Mia's bed and Mia's round brown shoulder was exposed. As she pulled Mia's sheet up, Jane saw a scrap of faded cotton quilt—Mia had secretly packed her old blankie, the blankie Jane had made for her when she was a baby. Jane smiled and bent to kiss Mia goodnight. As she inhaled the familiar drugstore odors of watermelon and strawberry in her daughter's hair, she smelled something else, bright and new, a sour trace of womanly sweat. She dropped the sheet and slipped back into her own bed, moving Mac as far over to the wall as she could.

The next morning Mac suggested they go snorkeling. It would be "a serious experience"—when had he started to talk this way?—and Mia would see all sorts of "outrageous" reef fish—she might even see a barracuda. Jane marveled again at his innocence as Mia predictably said, "No way." They drove to a black sand beach and Mia spread a towel out, plopped down, and closed her eyes, her box of unused tissues beside her. Jane picked up the huge book Mia had been reading. "Valdred parted the silken bed curtains and growled with blood lust at the sight of Delphia's pulsing purity." No wonder Mia felt sick, with garbage like that in her head. When had she stopped reading *Little House on the Prairie*? While Jane was off trying molestation cases? Trying to make enough money to pay their mortgage and buy their groceries?

She put the book down and sat hugging her knees. A solitary woman in a rusty black one-piece bathing suit stood waist-deep in the water, pulling a mask on over her face. Jane remembered snorkeling years ago, in Mexico, with college friends, the fun it had been, and after a while she picked up her own mask and snorkel and followed the other swimmer into the ocean.

It was still fun. The shallows flickered with bright butterfly fish, wrasse, and parrotfish, and the sound of her own breathing through the tube was intimate and encouraging. At first she stayed in the shallows, but something sweet, slow, and shadowy drew her deeper and she saw to her delight that she was only inches from a large sea turtle, his mild eyes and mossy beak guiding her silently through a boulder garden studded with corals. Hidden underwater, she relaxed her vigilance. How safe and peaceful it was down here! She swept soundlessly into the warm currents, her hands opening wide to wing her forward. Silver bubbles broke as the woman in the black suit splashed ahead, leading her out deeper and deeper. I could stay down here forever, Jane thought, and the desire to do just that startled her so that she surfaced with a kick and struck for shore. She was just in time to see Mac on his knees looming over Mia's bare back, tenderly applying sun block. Neither looked up as Jane dripped toward them. At the other end of the beach, the woman in the black suit emerged from the surf and pulled off her mask, releasing a cloud of white hair as she snatched up a small dog and crabbed off toward the parking lot.

"Pele's here," Jane said.

"Someone you know?" Mac asked.

Jane stared after the woman, then squatted down on her towel and groped through her bag for the guidebook. "Pele," she read out loud, "vengeful goddess of the volcano, often appears in the guise of an old woman with a white dog. She can often be seen hitch hiking along the highway. She lives deep inside the Kilauea Crater and accepts offerings at its rim; she is said to be particularly fond of cigarettes and gin."

Mia turned her head, eyes closed. "What's she vengeful about?" Mia asked.

"Her lover was a pig god," Jane explained. "And one day, when Pele was visiting another island, he seduced her younger sister."

Mia made a pretty face and arched her back. "Yick. Pig god."

"Oh, they're not a bad sort." Mac capped the sun block lotion. "Once you get to know them."

"She roasted him on a spit, served him at a luau, turned her sister into a pineapple, and had her canned," Jane improvised.

"Right. And you just saw her."

"I see her all the time. She's everywhere."

Everywhere was intolerable and every day got worse. They went to the City of Refuge, where early Hawaiians had fled to escape the wrath of their kings, and Mac said wouldn't it be nice to live in a place like that, outside the law, where you could do anything you liked, with whomever you wanted. They went to a sacred altar at the tip of the island where King Kamehameha had been born, and as Jane frowned at the rough carved birthing stone, Mac picked flowers for Mia's backpack. They drove to the Palolu Valley Lookout and while Jane photographed the view, Mac photographed Mia.

On and on it went. Mac wooed Mia and Mia sniffled and read her book and Jane was sad and mad and hurt and could not show it because—what was the point? What could she do? If she spelled out the obvious she would ruin everyone's vacation; if she simply sat on her feelings she would only ruin her own. On the next to last night, after a romantic sunset dinner at the guidebook's favorite restaurant, where, instead of asking Jane to marry him, Mac raised his mai tai and said, "To Mia's first time in Hawaii, may there be many more," Jane pleaded a headache and walked off by herself. Mia wasn't in danger. Mac would never rape her. He loved her too much to harm her. Jane had never had anyone love her that much. Had anyone ever loved her at all? Mia's father, for a while. Mia herself, for a while.

Wearily, drearily, Jane drifted through crowds of tourists and locals, stopping at a grocery store for a bottle of gin, not even minding that the old woman who sold it to her had white hair and an ancient Jack Russell asleep on a straw mat. When she passed the huge banyan tree, she ducked and went in.

It was a hideous tree, with its dangling gray vines and ridged roots intersecting in haphazard connections. It was dim and musty inside and seemed wild with invisible bird life. Jane sat down, drank straight from the bottle, and looked up at the crazy web over her head. It seemed that anything that wanted to could grow here, in any direction. It was like Hawaii itself, she decided, with its easy philosophy of acceptance. Under this tree, everything was possible, everything was permitted. A middle-aged man in love with a thirteen-year-old girl? No problem. A jealous mother hallucinating goddesses? Welcome. Everyone was welcome here. For a while. And then the tree gave out, gave up, had to, died. It could only accept so much, because so much was unacceptable.

On their last day they went to the crater. They had already gone to see the lava spill at the sea, the thin streams of red pouring over the black rock, the dramatic puffs of steam as fire hit the waves. But Kilauea itself, Mac said, was something to save for the end. Things worth having, he said, were worth waiting for. He gave a brave false wink to Jane as he said this, as if willing her to think he was referring to sex, sex with her, which had not happened all week and would probably never happen again. "You seem distant," he said, glancing at her as he drove. She nodded without answering. They had entered the rainforest at the base of the volcano. Yellow ginger and royal purple princess plants tumbled over each other in jungle profusion, crowding out the older native foliage around them. Mac turned the radio up—rap music—and said over his shoulder to Mia, "Do you dig this, sweetie?" but Mia, in the backseat, had her headphones on. She hadn't said anything except the usual, "I don't feel good," since breakfast.

"I don't dig it," Jane said. "If you care what I dig."

"Of course I do." Mac clicked the radio off. They curved up the Crater Rim Road and started through the lava fields. It was a new landscape up here, totally different from the flowering green jungles below, a high vast plain of pewter-colored rubble pocked with cracks and crevices of smoke. Jane watched a frigate bird soar through the warm gray air over the lifeless plateau and took in a shallow sniff of sulphur, then another, its dark eggy odor weighting her lungs. Her throat felt crowded with short hot bad words; her eyes burned; her pulse twitched. When they came to the end of the road, she turned to Mia.

"Want to come see where Pele lives?"

"I can see it from here." Mia turned a page of her book.

"Mac?"

"I'll stay with Mia."

"Not if I can help it." Jane heard her voice break and saw her face reflected in Mac's sunglasses. This tense, tight-lipped woman was his girlfriend? No wonder he preferred the daughter. Who wouldn't? She got out alone, slammed the door, and started up the path.

The air smelled of sewage and the loose lava tinkled like glass beneath her feet as she climbed to the top. Offerings to the goddess crusted the rim of the crater: sea shells, coins wrapped in ti leaves, cigarettes, dried leis. She crouched to set her own offerings down: the half-empty bottle of gin, the guidebook. She straightened and stared into the great smoky hollow, which was, as she knew it would be, empty. An empty socket that stared blindly back at all who stared blindly in. Nothing there. Never had been. It was tempting to give a great roar and spread her arms and jump in, incinerating with rage as she dropped to the bottom. Tempting too to turn aside and hold on to this rage, to let it smolder as she grew older and angrier and more and more bitter. She glanced over her shoulder at the rental car in the parking lot. Mia's pale face shone in the back seat and Mac was a large shadow slumped over the steering wheel. They looked alone, unconnected, and almost—she hesitated—asleep? She could see Mia's hands folded against her cheek, pressed to the window, Mac's big shoulders rising and falling in rhythmic slumber.

Is it possible, Jane thought, that I've been the only one awake this whole trip? She waited, braced for a breath of rude laughter. But the crater was silent. She started back toward the car and got in. "We were worried about you, Mom," Mia said, stretching, "you were gone so long." Mac nodded, yawned, and started the engine. Silently, they drove down the long loop of the grey mountain road. As they took the last curve, they passed an old woman bouncing in the back of a pickup truck driven by two bare-chested island boys. Her baseball cap was askew on her wiry white hair, her muumuu billowed, her dog barked from her lap, and her eyes glowed like hot coals. She grinned straight at Jane with her toothless mouth and waved. Jane, turning to watch her recede, saw a thin flow of lava begin to pour from the pierced heart of the mountain. By the time they reached town it had diminished to a simple line of moonlight and when they flew home the next morning it was nothing but haze on the ocean. Still, Jane knew it was there. She would always know it was there.

FIVE MINUTES OF MADNESS

Becka worked until midnight helping Danny frame his pictures, and during all that time did Jen show up at the studio? Did Jen phone, did Jen drop off a hot casserole, did Jen so much as offer to order them a pizza? She did not. Jen stayed home with a headache and watched *Moulin Rouge*. Becka could not believe that a wife would flake out like that when her husband had a big art opening the very next day. It was crazy. It was lazy. But you had to say one thing: it was just like Jen.

Danny was so tired that he was swaying as he hung the last painting, and Becka had to help him down off the ladder. "You better stay here with me tonight," she warned, but Danny said no, he'd be fine, and Becka watched him limp across the warehouse parking lot to his truck. She frowned because no matter what he said, Danny was not "fine"; he was run down and needed a complete physical. But when was he going to find time to see a doctor? It wasn't enough that he had to squander his genius working at the Art Institute. He also had to shop and cook and clean house and garden and walk the dog and rent movies, and why? To keep Jen from getting depressed.

Depressed!

Becka turned off the lights, locked up, and went to bed. As usual, she had a hard time sleeping. It could get creepy in the Industrial Building at night. Drunks wandered down from the Sausalito bars and bums scrounged through the dumpsters, and every now and then a cop car cruised through, radio barking, and she had to hold her breath because she wasn't supposed to be living here in the first place; Danny was letting her stay only until she found a job. But how could she find a job when she had so much to do right here? The gallery that offered to hire her wanted her six full days a week—she'd never have time to stretch Danny's canvases the way he liked—and the architects' office insisted that she show up at nine. Nine was when Danny needed his latte.

Danny was such a child—he didn't even know how much he needed those lattes. He always looked so surprised. Alone on her cot in the dark, Becka muffled a laugh, remembering Danny's wide eyes, his parted lips, the way his cowlick stuck up as he breathed in the milky steam from the cup and said, "Why thank you, Becka. What a treat."

Did Jen ever "treat" him? Did Jen ever listen to his dreams or read funny tidbits out of the paper or find exactly the right radio station or keep the welder next door from making too much noise or the potter down the hall from messing up the latrine? Did Jen ever trim his curls or sew the buttons on his shirt? Did Jen ever sleep with him?

Becka closed her eyes. Some things did not bear thinking about.

The next morning, Becka went out on her bike but she was back with last minute supplies, hours before the opening, and was Jen there then? Surprise: She was not. Becka put down Danny's latte, smacked a cranberry/bran/walnut muffin down beside it and said, "Well, I'll tell you one thing, my friend. If this is marriage, count me out."

Danny lifted his soft wide eyes and said, "I'd never count you out."

Becka flushed, sniffed, glanced at the time and got to work. There was the card table to set up, wine glasses to wash and set out, the flowers to arrange. "Is that wife of yours even awake?" she asked.

"Oh I'm sure she is. She's going to bring the wine and beer," Danny said.

"How about the cheese and crackers?"

"I think she's doing that too."

"You think?"

Danny turned to her and smiled. "Don't worry," he said.

"I just don't want anything to go wrong for you today." Becka wiped her hands on her jeans and looked around the studio. She'd swept the concrete floor, knocked the spider webs off the rafters. She'd washed the high windows, scrubbed the latrine. The place shone and the walls, hung with Danny's canvases, actually glowed. For the last year Danny had been painting a series of crystal gazing balls—luminescent green and red and purple globes with frail images like ghost fish swimming inside. All the paintings had titles: "Fortunate Stranger," "Fear of a Fair Child," "Travel Over Winter Water." Becka's favorite, a blue globe that blazed like a hot sapphire moon, was titled "Five Minutes of Madness." Sometimes, standing before it, Becka could feel her heart flood, her blood fizz, her lungs levitate. The blue was so pure, the core of the gazing ball so radiant. She could not talk about this. It was just the way Danny's paintings affected her. She smiled and placed a vase of white roses on a low table before the guest book.

Her smile tightened and trembled as the first guests arrived. They were early, but even so—where were the wine and beer? Where was the ice? Where were the cheese and crackers? Where, in other words, was Jen? Becka, as usual, had to be the hostess, showing people around the studio while Danny stood to one side, talking to a few of his students in his usual friendly way. Several people thought Becka was Danny's wife—that always happened. It was partly, Becka knew, because she and Danny, after seeing each other every day for the last eleven months, had started to look alike, with their short gray curls and thin shoulders. Sometimes, without meaning to, they even dressed alike; today, for instance, both were wearing black tee shirts and black jeans.

Half an hour later, lo and behold, Lady Jen Herself, in a yellow cotton sundress that was too short for her fat legs, arrived with a box—could you believe it?—a *box* of white wine and two six packs of cheap beer and no red wine at all.

"What am I supposed to do with this?" Becka asked as Jen plunked the grocery bags down on the table.

"Oh look," Jen said, as if that were an answer. "There's my yoga teacher."

And she wandered off. No yoga teacher had been on the guest list or on the invitations that Becka had designed, handwritten, and mailed three weeks ago. That list had been tailored for buyers, people with money who knew something about art. These people crowding the studio now were nobodies, people Jen knew from her hairdresser's or the dog park. Becka heard the Neil Young she had put on especially for Danny stop in mid-verse, replaced by Jen's Neil Diamond, and gritted her teeth. Opening the wine, she made sure that the names of the few invitees who had showed up were served first because, cheap as it was, wine helped sell paintings. She slipped price lists into pockets and purses, talked about Danny's development over the years and about the magic that imbued this new series of paintings. She was explaining the gazing ball to two young lawyers when Jen interrupted her.

"Becka?" Jen said, leading a giggly woman with fake nails with hearts on them by the hand. "This friend of mine wants to see the real thingy."

"What real thingy?"

"The real crystal ball. The one Daniel used in his paintings."

"It's not here. It's next door. It's mine." Becka turned back to the lawyers. "I bought it years ago at an antique shop in Berkeley. An old man there used it to predict my future."

"Could you go get it?" Jen asked.

"Say what?"

"Could. You. Go. Get. It."

"Becka?" Danny came up and touched her elbow as she stood staring at Jen. "A lot of people want to see that crystal ball. Would you mind stepping next door and bringing it out?"

Silent, Becka let herself out through the side door and into her room. It was small, a cell really, narrow and lightless. The walls were lined with half-finished sketches of Danny at work, on his stool under the skylight, listening to music, paint brush in hand. Her few clothes were hung on a line from the rafters; her soap and towel were laid beside the utility sink. The crystal ball, inert and dull as a light bulb, sat on top of a file cabinet. It was nothing without the infusion of radiance that Danny's vision gave it. When she reached for it and drew it close, it reflected her face, which surprised her. She hadn't seen herself mirrored like this since she'd bought the ball years ago, when she was the star of the art department, a young girl with a bright future. How pale and pinched she looked now! She remembered the old man's prediction. "You will never have fame or fortune," he had told her. "But you will have something else. You will have a great love."

She picked up the ball in both hands—it was light—and turned to go back. Through the half-open door she heard Jen's voice, that affected laugh of hers, "No, no, I'm Danny's wife," Jen was saying. "Becka's just a squatter here."

Squatter? I don't think so, Becka thought. She entered the studio, clasping the ball, said, "Here it is. Catch," and threw it. She watched, unsurprised, as Jen jumped aside and covered her face. The ball shattered on the cement floor, shooting out sharp rainbow fragments that arrowed toward the leaping legs of the guests. Jen was harpooned in a dozen tiny places and screamed predictably as blood pearled from her fat white legs.

"Becka?" Danny said. He looked at her in wonder. "Why did you do that?"

"You don't know?"

"I can't imagine." And he turned from her and bent over Jen, who couldn't even bleed right, who had in fact stopped bleeding altogether, who was already starting to laugh.

"Oh Daniel," Jen said. "Go get the broom."

Becka started to say, No Danny, Don't Worry Danny, Let Me Do It Danny, but she didn't. She didn't say a word. She just walked out of the studio into the glaring afternoon and marched down toward the wharf at the end of the parking lot. She could still see the gazing ball's shattered glass geyser shooting up like fireworks over the ocean and the city beyond and hear Jen's screams repeated by the seagulls overhead. She opened her own mouth and screamed. It felt good. It felt great. She screamed again and again until Danny's quiet voice behind her said, "Becka?" Then she turned.

Her five minutes were up.

SYMPTOMS

PRIVATELY SHE THOUGHT HER DOCTOR might have left something in, a needle or one of his tools. She could not take a deep breath or sleep on her left side. The pain was supposed to go away but it didn't and she spent a lot of time trying to describe it in her mind. She wanted to be precise when she had her follow-up on Tuesday and she did not want Dr. Azam to think she was accusing him of negligence or even mildly suggesting a lawsuit. She would simply tell Dr. Azam that it wasn't the "dull ache" he'd said she'd feel after the hysterectomy, no, this was different. This felt foreign. Hard. Hostile. This felt like something inside wanted to kill her.

Which was crazy. The idea of a famous surgeon leaving a clamp, or a knife, or whatever they used—a staple gun? a small pair of scissors!—inside a patient—that never could happen. Dr. Azam was the best GYN in Atlanta and she trusted him completely. Her husband Royal was his financial advisor after all and surely Dr. Azam would know better than to antagonize his own financial advisor. So unless Royal had a beautiful young mistress he wanted to marry and Dr. Azam had taken a bribe and agreed to help him out by making her, Betsy, a stone cold corpse and Royal an eligible widower . . . Stop it.

Stop. It.

This all came from the trash she'd been reading in bed. Murder mysteries. Blood. Gore. Dead wives everywhere. She should be reading the Russian novels that her book group was discussing but it was hard to concentrate on anything as complicated as Russia when her side hurt so badly. Husbands in the books she read killed their wives on yachts, on rooftops, in deserted warehouses. They dragged them by their hair, drowned them in their baths, threw them over balconies. So many men hated women.

Of course Royal did not hate her. He loved her. He loved her despite her trifocals, short grey curls, chipmunk cheeks. She still had good skin, thank goodness, and her neck hadn't collapsed altogether, but she had put on weight. Last night Royal had laughed about a colleague who was sleeping with a morbidly obese client, and Betsy had said, without thinking, "You have your own little fat woman to sleep with," and he'd said, "I know," which was not the right thing to say. But that was all right. She would lose weight as soon as she felt better. She would go to the gym, walk on a regular basis with her good friend Julia, maybe even try tennis again. Or no. Yoga. Though she hated the sight of her baggy knees creeping creepily down when she lifted her legs for the headstand. And the way she had started to quietly fart in class when doing Downward Dog.

Downward Dog was Royal's favorite position for sex and she would have to ask Dr. Azam about that too, about sex, that is; Royal wanted her to bring it up at her appointment on Tuesday, and she would, though she did not really see the point. It wasn't as if she could ever have another child, and she would probably never even have a grandchild, not with Chrissy in San Francisco dead set on a career in film making and Chad showing up every Thanksgiving with another new girlfriend. "Our children are middle-aged," Royal kept repeating last Thanksgiving, and she could tell Chad and Chrissy had been hurt, which was perhaps one reason why they hadn't phoned once since she'd been home from the hospital, assuming, like everyone else, she was fine.

But she wasn't fine. Something bad was inside her. Maybe an overlooked renegade cancer, sharp and pronged as coral, branching out swiftly in its new dark space. Maybe one of the nurses had lost an earring or maybe Dr. Azam's wedding ring had slipped into her insides when he stripped his gloves off.

Ridiculous.

Anyway, did Muslims even wear wedding rings?

How long had he been in this country anyway?

Who knew where he'd gone to medical school! Pakistan? Tehran? Baghdad? Maybe he'd planted a grenade inside her! Any time he chose, he could push a button and she and all her friends would blow up!

Take a pill.

Take another.

She had too much time to think; that was the problem. Lately she had been thinking about the past, silly things, small. Summers with her grandmother in the country, a train trip to Memphis. One incident recurred to her again and again. It was 1957, that autumn day when the young black man appeared out of nowhere and walked right up the front steps of the high school as if he was going to class with the rest of them and without a word all the boys separated out and silently followed him up the stairs. She and the other girls waited in the courtyard below. It was shameful to admit this now, but all she had known at the time was that she didn't want the whole school to be closed down. After a while the boys started flowing down the stairs again. And the young black man? It was all right. He wasn't a student. He was just the new bus driver.

Dr. Azam wasn't black, exactly, so she didn't know why she kept coming back to this memory over and over. There were so many ways of looking at things! Why couldn't she just pretend that her pain was the bus driver: a misguided visitor? Not meant to stay.

Tuesday came and she went to her appointment. It was odd because that day for some perverse reason nothing hurt. Dr. Azam pressed here, pressed there—nothing. Not even that dull ache he had predicted. She was healing perfectly, Dr. Azam said. She was his prize patient.

So that night she let Royal pull her nightgown up and roll her over and it wasn't too painful as long as she did not move to her left side. And it was worth it just for the relief it brought him. His deep laugh of gratification as he held her afterward was payment enough, not that payment was the right word.

"You all right, Bets?" he asked sleepily, and she said Yes, yes she was but she thought she would read for a moment if he didn't mind. "Read to me?" he asked. "Your voice always puts me right out." Which was tactless, but not intended to hurt. Royal never meant to hurt. Most men didn't. Not even Julia's husband who insisted on talking about Julia's masectomy at parties but never remembered which breast it was. How often had Julia in a hushed voice had to say, "Not the left one, Hoyt. The right one." Compared to Julia, she was lucky. Compared to everyone she was lucky.

She read a chapter about a murder on a cruise ship, closed the book after Royal started to snore and turned off the light. She rolled without thinking to her left. The pain was so sudden that she pressed her face to the pillow and for no reason at all started to cry.

THE DELIGHT

Many of Doc's writing students returned year after year just to see him. They came back to be married in his garden, dance in his living room, visit with his wife Sue in his kitchen, or simply sit and sip whiskey on his front porch and listen all night to his long, funny, frankly profane stories. Some dedicated their poems to him, a few even named their babies after him, but Jamie Day was the only student who had ever come back to cook a meal for him, and Doc wasn't sure what to make of that. The only thing he recalled Jamie cooking in the past was hash. From Morocco.

Jamie had said he'd arrive at five and at five Doc, who had grown up in the country and told time by the sun, set down his beer, closed his book, and rose from his rocking chair in wonder. Jamie had been late to every seminar Doc had ever taught, had slept through his oral exam, missed his own graduation. But here he came now, four years later, stepping smartly up the garden path. He still had the wavy hair, pointy elf ears, and slim torso that had made half the girls and a few of the boys in the MFA program fall for him, but instead of the flowing silk scarves and scuffed cowboy boots he was wearing a dress shirt and pressed jeans and there was something strained in his face that Doc didn't recognize. Perhaps it was the smile, bright and brisk, or the tight grip he kept on the cloth bag of groceries, or the intent way he listened to the cell phone pressed to his cheek.

"Everything all right?" Doc asked.

"Are you kidding? Things have never been better!" Jamie bounded up the unpainted porch steps and bumped his head against his old professor's shoulder twice. "Sweetie?" He said into the phone. "You wouldn't believe it. Doc's just the same. Still drinking Red Rock. Yes. Still reading Dante."

"Who the fuck are you talking to?" Doc asked.

"Zanthe. Do you want to say hello to her?"

"No. I want to say hello to you. Hang the hell up."

"Don't you love his voice? Deep. Southern. Okay sweetie. Bye." Jamie pressed his phone shut. "Zanthe's my girlfriend, " he explained. "She's beautiful."

Doc nodded. Jamie had always had girlfriends and they had always been beautiful. "Blonde?"

"How did you know?"

"Zanthe means 'golden.'"

"I forgot," Jamie said humbly. "You know Greek. You know everything. Hey! If I'm cooking dinner tonight, guess I'd better start! Is the gang coming? That's what Zanthe calls my friends here. The James Gang."

"Most of your friends left town four years ago," Doc pointed out. "But we rounded up a few stragglers." He turned to lead the way into the house, stopped in the doorway, chuckled. It was good to see Jamie again, for despite his bad manners and salesman's smile, something about the boy seemed as sweet and eager to please as ever. "We've missed you," Doc said. "It's been pretty damn dull here since you left. Matt Baker's still talking about the time he found your pet snake in his bathtub. " He paused. "You okay with seeing Matt tonight? He's married now, has a baby."

"Zanthe and I aren't ready for babies."

"Indeed. Well, come on into the kitchen. I'll get you a beer."

"No thanks. I don't drink."

"Since when?"

"I never did drink. I mean I *drank*. Just not like the rest of you."

"Right. You drank more than the rest of us."

"I did?"

"You don't remember?"

"I don't hold on to negative memories. Gosh it's great to be back here. Sweetie?"

The phone again? Doc shook his head, opened the refrigerator and reached for another beer.

"You wouldn't believe the books in this house, sweetie. We are talking floor to ceiling, room after room. Yeah, I know it's a lot of trees. But he's read every one of them. Sometimes twice! Doc, Zanthe wants to know: how many books do you read a week?"

"Not enough," Doc said, taking a long sip.

"He probably reads twenty books a week. Okay, sweetie, I know. It's late. I'll get started." Still clutching the bag of groceries, Jamie took in the familiar plaid wallpaper, curling posters of Rembrandt, Dürer, and Elvis, the white enamel appliances and windowsills crammed with Sue's pots of basil and parsley. He paused before the framed photos of Doc as a high school quarterback, as an Army medic, accepting a prize for his first book, shaking hands with Robert Penn Warren. He read the song titles from the antique jukebox and hummed a few bars of "Jackson." He peered at the photo of Sue dancing at Woodstock and frowned at a snapshot of himself and Evie Brandt kissing here, in this kitchen, years ago.

"I told Zanthe about Evie," he said. "We have no secrets. Hope you're hungry!" He set the grocery sack down and it promptly fell over, spilling bunches of kale, chard, spinach, mustard greens, dandelion greens, cucumbers, a damp wedge of tofu, a bag of brown noodles, a bouquet of hairy carrots and a large pale cabbage onto the wooden table.

Doc whistled.

"I know," Jamie agreed. "It's a lot. But it's all sustainable. I hope you have cast iron pots."

"We have all sorts of pots. We even have some pot-pot if you want it."

Somehow, somewhere, Jamie Day had learned to look shocked. "I sure don't," he said. "Of course if you . . ."

Doc lifted his beer in a stilling salute and watched as Jamie went to the sink and began scrubbing his hands.

"I can't believe it," Jamie said. "It's like I never went away."

"So let's hear it. Where *did* you go?" Doc handed Jamie the utensils he needed as Jamie told him how the New York thing hadn't worked out and then the Thailand thing hadn't worked out and then the Seattle thing hadn't worked out and then this amazing thing, in Los Angeles of all places, had worked out—and that thing was Zanthe. "Pow!" Jamie said, his eyes tearing as he hacked at an onion.

"Pow?" Sue, home from her job at the courthouse, came in through the screen door, arms held out. Doc knew Jamie was one of Sue's pets. Jamie's sad history—no father, mother in and out of mental hospitals, brother in jail—had won him a solid place in her heart. Plus she had always liked his poems. Jamie had turned in loopy sonnets about his adventures in foster care and juvenile detention centers, and Sue, who read all of Doc's students' work, thought they made a lively change from the careful stanzas the other students turned in. "My," she said now, when Jamie stepped forward to kiss her on both cheeks. "You used to goose me. When did you learn to kiss so sweet? And what happened to all your fancy piercings? And your blue streaked ponytail tied up with condoms? You're wearing Ralph Lauren! What's goin' on, darlin'? Are you in love?"

Jamie, eyes brimming, nodded. "I am," he said, gripping Sue's hands. "I am in love."

"That's wonderful," Sue beamed. "Is she a good person?"

"Zanthe's the best thing that ever happened to me," Jamie said. "Oops, excuse me, here she is now. Sweetie? Yes. I know. I'm draining the tofu the way you taught me."

"That's the third time she's phoned," Doc pointed out.

"Shush you," Sue said. "This Zanthe sounds great. He needed a manager." She took the glass of red wine Doc poured her, and went to the door as the bell rang.

Matt Baker was the first to arrive. He brought Emma Jane, aged eight months, strapped to his back. Evie Brandt followed close behind, wearing bright red lipstick and tight black jeans, hand in hand with the newest Fiction Fellow, a tall Canadian named Brick, and a few seconds later they were joined by Jamie's old poetry slam rivals, Tess and Reed. They all clumped in the doorway, waiting to say hello while Jamie continued to talk on the phone, his back turned to them.

"Why won't he say hi?" Brick asked.

"Guilt," Matt guessed.

"Because?"

"Because four years ago he crashed Evie's motorcycle, lost Tess's dog, ruined Reed's piano and set fire to my thesis."

"On purpose?"

"No, Jamie never did anything on purpose. Everything he did was accidental."

"Even your thesis?"

"I was trying to write like Kerouac," Matt explained. "You know, typing on a single scroll of butcher paper?"

"And Jamie was . . .?"

"Practicing his flame juggling. He apologized in tears afterwards and since then he's been too embarrassed to talk to me."

"Who's he talking to now?"

"A new girlfriend," Tess guessed.

"I was his old girlfriend," Evie said.

"You were my old girlfriend too," Reed reminded her.

And almost mine as well, Doc thought, remembering the April afternoon when Evie had come into his office, burst into tears, and pressed her breasts against him. He had disengaged himself from her then, ruffling her hair and comforting her like a fond father; he was not sure he would behave so well now. Something had happened to him these last few months, some renegade randiness that he had successfully suppressed through his long years of teaching had come to the surface; he found himself lusting after dull sorority girls, obsessing about the little blonde blusher in his Keats and Shelley class, flirting with the department secretary. He supposed it had something to do with turning sixty, to having his last two books rejected, to watching Sue age—she no longer even tried to diet—or perhaps to the daily drain of dealing with his elderly mother—who knew.

He opened a bottle of Jack Daniels and passed it around and they all watched Evie sway boldly forward to tap Jamie on the shoulder. Jamie turned with that tight bright smile, accepted the kiss she placed on his lips, waved cheerfully to the others, and kept on talking. Evie gave an exaggerated shrug and returned to Brick. "I'm all yours," she said. "Again."

"It must be weird for him, being back here with all of us tonight," Tess said, "I mean, the way he left, both legs broken. He jumped off Doc's roof on graduation night," she explained to Brick. "Oh," she added, "look what I brought." She reached into her purse and pulled out a fat stick of salami. Everyone laughed. "Remember how Jamie used to shove salami inside his shorts when he taught Freshman Comp? He said it was the only way he knew to keep the undergrads' attention."

But now, after he turned off his phone, was introduced to Brick, shook hands with Reed, ignored Matt Baker, kiss-kissed Tess, tried to kiss-kiss Evie, who, with a queenly gesture, turned her head aside, all Jamie said about the salami was, "Dead animals? I don't eat dead animals. Of course," he added earnestly, "I don't care if the rest of you do. I'm open to other cultural climates. Like when I was teaching in Thailand? Everything was cooked with dead animals. I got tired of eating just the rice around the dead animals, so I did eat dead animals when I was in Thailand. Gosh, it's great to see everyone, it really is, and I can't wait to catch up, but would you mind sitting outside while I get this dinner together? Zanthe says I need to focus."

"Well if Zanthe says," Evie sang childishly under her breath.

"Oops! Phone. Sweetie? Yes, just about to rinse the kale. Yes, in the sink. Doc? Do you know if your tap water is pure? He says it's pure as donkey piss, no, that's just his sense of humor. Please don't hang up. Oh boy. Now she's hung up on me."

"Good," Matt said. "Come on out to the porch and have a cigarette with us."

"He doesn't smoke," Doc guessed.

"I never did," Jamie smiled. "I mean," when everyone turned to look at him, "not like you guys."

"If I called Sue that often," Doc said, as they all settled onto the porch and lit up, "She'd think I was having an affair."

"Actually," Sue said, "You did use to call me all the time. You used to read me your poems on the phone."

"Thirty-eight years ago," Doc drawled. "Anyone going to help me with this whiskey?"

They all held their glasses out and tried not to wince as something shattered in the kitchen, followed by three heavy bumps and a crash. "We could spend the time telling Jamie stories," Sue suggested.

They did. Evie told the Jamie-arrested-for-drunk-walking story, Reed told the Jamie-arrested-for-drunk-crawling story, Tess told the Jamie-arrested-for-drunk-naked-break-dancing story and Matt told about the time Jamie came home with the old woman he had found camping down by the river and fed for three days until she wandered off again. Everyone remembered the boa in the bathtub and the ten thousand dollar jackpot at the Indian casino, and how Jamie had given every cent of it away to the church by the rail yards, and everyone but Doc remembered graduation night, when Jamie had jumped off the roof. "Was he trying to kill himself?" Brick asked, amazed.

"He said he wasn't. He said he jumped on a dare."

"Who would dare him to do something like that?"

"We all would," Matt said.

"We were pretty bad," Evie agreed. "We knew he'd do just about anything you asked him to."

"I always thought he was trying to impress Doc that night," Tess said.

"Me?" Doc was surprised. "He could have impressed me by turning his work in on time."

"He loved you." Evie's voice was matter-of-fact. "You were the one he loved."

"Dumb way of showing it." Doc reached for the bottle and refilled his glass. He had no memory of that party or of Jamie's accident. That night was lost to him—ten hours without sound or light—but he monitored his drinking better these days and hadn't had a blackout in months. Tonight, he could tell, would be fine; the whiskey was working the way it was supposed to, carrying him along on an easy, happy, downriver float. The young faces around him were lit like lilies and he flushed with affection for all of them. He chuckled, put one arm around Brick and one around Reed and began to tell a long story about a free-diving Cajun his uncle Dooley knew who had tried to give mouth-to-mouth to a catfish he was convinced had the bends.

"Dinner," Jamie called, from inside the house. Matt stood and waved Emma Jane's hands up and down—"Past her bedtime," Matt explained—and disappeared through the garden. The others stepped into chaos. Pots, pans, bowls, and utensils were stacked on every surface of the kitchen. The table in the dining room had been cleared of Doc's books and papers and set with his mother's hand-painted china. Each plate contained a heap of pale brown and dark green foods, decorated with a cross of cooked cucumber on top like a Confederate flag. Jamie, beaming, waved them in. "Doc, you sit here," he said, pulling a chair out at the end of the table for Doc. "And Matt here . . ."

"Matt's gone home," Evie said.

"Oh no! I wanted to give him the seat of honor next to Doc."

"Why? You wouldn't speak to him. You hate him."

"I do? Matt Baker?"

"He has a tenure-track job, a gorgeous wife, a beautiful baby, and a new book coming out next spring. We all hate him," Reed said.

"I don't hate anyone," Jamie protested. "Except people who do bad things. And then I don't hate the people. I just hate the bad things."

No one could think of anything to say to that. Silent, they all sat and looked at their plates. Finally Evie said, "What is it?"

"It's a dish Zanthe and I, well, mostly Zanthe, invented. It's essentially tofu with greens and carrageenan all cooked down with amino acid."

"Did he say amino acid?" Brick whispered.

"You could use soy sauce," Jamie continued. "But Zanthe and I like to use amino acid. And then if we want to make it fancy, we add a little garlic."

"Did you want to make it fancy?" Reed asked.

"I did. I added a little garlic. We call it 'The Delight.'"

They all took a bite.

"There's something else in here," Tess said.

"Buttermilk."

"Doc's Aunt Ora put buttermilk in everything," Sue said, to break the silence.

"Ora's cooking was so bad you'd want to lick a dog's ass just to get the taste out of your mouth," Doc added. There was laughter, then silence again as everyone looked down at their plates.

"Hey Jamie." Reed's voice was a little too loud. "Remember Kiernan Whelan? Big guy? Kept getting bigger? Took steroids? He married Amber Dillard who was with Jonas McMann who was with Shannon Hammond who was with Travis Guy who was with—"

"Me!" Tess crowed.

"Anyway he and Amber teach in Colorado now."

"Were we all crazy?" Jamie asked.

"Why?"

"The way we slept around back then? Like no one really mattered. Like we were all disposable. Zanthe says—"

"I never felt disposable," Evie interrupted, "and Kiernan Whelan was an all right guy. Except he did kiss up to that crazy redhead professor from England."

"The Living Statue," Tess nodded. "She was awful. I took her Form and Theory class and she gave me a B."

"Oh no, baby got a B," Reed mocked.

"I don't mind getting a B if I deserve it, really I don't but I had done all the work and I had worked hard. So I went in to see her because I'm so . . ."

"Anal," Reed said.

"Yes, and because when I don't do well I like to know why. So I went to her office and she opened her grade book and said, Well, I gave Tandy Evans an A because her mother died in April and I gave LeVon Johnson an A because

LeVon you know was in a gang and I think it's just so wonderful that he's not on the streets any more and I gave Jay McPhail an A because he was in a car accident and I gave Jamie Day an A because . . ."

"Jay McPhail?" Jamie said. "Wow. I remember him. He said terrible things in workshop, didn't he? Really rude."

"Yes," Reed agreed. "He told me my poems were 'country cute'."

"He read everything I wrote out loud in falsetto," Evie said.

"Why were we so mean to each other?" Jamie asked.

"Were we?"

"When I tell Zanthe about our old workshops she can't believe it. All that pointless sarcasm? Zanthe says—"

"Oh hush up about Zanthe," Evie said. "You used to talk about William Blake and Denis Johnson and Nick Flynn and now all you talk about is Zanthe."

"I'm sorry." Jamie ducked his head. "It's just . . . she's worth talking about."

There was silence for a few minutes while everyone pushed their forks around, not eating, heads down. Doc looked at their sad faces and felt the evening darken around him. What kind of a party was this? The river of low laughter he'd been riding all night had abruptly stranded him on a gravel bank. He looked at Jamie's bent head with its neatly combed hair and felt a tingle of dislike. Who was this dull prig? And what had he done with the boy they all loved?

"Why?" he asked quietly into the silence.

"Why what?" Jamie asked.

"Why is Zanthe worth talking about?"

"Because she's wonderful and amazing and fantastic."

"Why?" Doc repeated.

"Use specifics," Tess reminded Jamie. "Pretend we're in class."

"Show-Don't-Tell," the others chimed. Evie leaned forward and touched Jamie's arm. "It's called meter, shithead," she whispered, quoting Doc's famous advice to beginners. "God's in the details," Reed agreed. "Tell us the details. Like for instance, what's her bra size?"

"Could we talk about something else?" Jamie said. "I don't feel this is appropriate."

"We just want to know if she's good enough for you," Sue soothed, but Doc interrupted with a loud "Hell no, we just want to know who she *is*. Who *is* this person, Jamie?"

"She's my savior," Jamie said. "Before I met her, I was . . . well you guys know what I was like." He looked up with that brain-dead smile. "She helped me find myself. My real self." Everyone stilled and even Doc, for a second, felt touched, but something still sparked in him—irritation with Jamie's naivete, perhaps. Jamie had always been a good student, open to wonder, receptive to beauty, truth, and every flavor of horseshit, but clearly, in this Zanthe, he'd found a bad teacher. Annoyed, Doc rose to look for something in the liquor cabinet as the others continued to ask Jamie about his girl friend. Nothing Doc heard reassured him—Zanthe owned the business where Jamie worked as a courier, she was six years older, ran marathons, had regular colonics, didn't read books or go to movies, thought Jamie had wasted his time in graduate school, discouraged him from writing. "I remember when we burned my poems," Jamie was saying. "We made this ceremony? Way out in the desert? Wish I could remember our chant. It went *Om mani pa* . . ."

"Would someone please stop him?" Evie said.

Doc straightened up from the liquor cabinet with the bottle of vintage moonshine he'd been looking for, rubbed the twinge in his back, found seven mismatched jelly jars, splashed a few inches of the moonshine into each of them and set the biggest one down in front of Jamie's plate.

"Son," he said, his voice the deep rumble his students tried and failed to imitate. "It was damn decent of you to come back and cook for us tonight and I'd like to propose a toast to the woman who made it all possible. Let's all drink to Zanthe."

"Really?" Jamie said, "I haven't had a drink in thirteen months. I don't think . . ."

"Don't think," Doc suggested. He placed one hand on Jamie's shoulder, looked into his uplifted eyes, and raised his jar in a friendly salute.

Jamie lifted his own jar, shook his head, set it down.

"I can't," he smiled.

"Sure you can." Doc's voice deepened. He paused and in a low voice no one else could hear, added, "Scared?"

Jamie shot an injured look at him.

Doc shrugged and turned aside.

"Okay," Jamie said suddenly. "Just one." His smile gave no indication that he remembered that "Just One" had been his nickname in grad school.

Doc waited until Jamie took a short swallow. Then he toasted again. To Sue. To Evie. To Reed. To Brick. To Matt. He watched Jamie take swallow after swallow and then, in the same tender voice, he asked, "Son? Why did you come here tonight?"

"She thought I was ready," Jamie answered, startled.

"So let's show her you are." Doc raised his jar one last time and waited, patient, until Jamie raised his as well. "To Jamie's return," Doc said.

"Hear! hear!" the others cried. "To Jamie's return!"

Jamie, flushed, unhappy, clinked with everyone, finished his jar. Then, hand trembling, he reached, as Doc knew he would, for the rest of the bottle.

"Anyone for a cigarette?" Doc asked.

"Not me," Jamie slurred, as the others rose to follow Doc out to the porch.

"Up to you. By the way, I'll take this." Doc pocketed Jamie's cell phone before Jamie could protest and went outside. Evie stayed behind at the table, watching Jamie finish the rest of the bottle.

"How'd it feel to burn your poems?" she asked.

"They were really bad poems, Evie."

"Yes, but how did it feel?"

"Odd. I cried. But then after, you know, I felt free. Released. You should do it too, Evie, you'd be a new person."

"I don't want to be a new person," Evie said. "I like my old person."

"I like her too." Jamie's eyes met Evie's in a look that was almost, for a moment, the hot saucy hit she remembered. Then he raised his voice. "Doc! Dammit! You gonna give me a cigarette or not?"

"Come and get it," Doc said.

It was five the next morning before Doc finished cleaning up. He dried the last plate, hung the damp dishtowel on the kitchen rack and went outside to sweep the cigarette butts off the porch. The cabbage Jamie had forgotten to put in The Delight gleamed like a damp skull on the planks, surrounded by cardboard containers from take out rib and pizza joints. Empty beer and wine bottles lined the railing, the salami Jamie had half-gnawed lay on the swing, and *The Inferno* had fallen face down on the rocking chair. Doc picked it up and went back inside. Sue opened her eyes as he came into the bedroom. "Get him out of jail all right?" she asked.

"Yeah. Evie took him home with her."

"Poor Jamie."

"He'll be fine. You should have seen him romancing the desk clerk." Doc chuckled. It had been a good party. Good laughter, good talk. Tess had sung an old Irish ballad in her pure soprano, Brick had recited one of Doc's early poems by heart, Reed had played gospel on the piano in the pool hall, Evie had slipped her small hand inside his back pocket not once but twice, and Jamie had finally begun to smile like his "real self," which was shy and sly and wild and free. Doc chuckled again, unbuckled his belt, and dropped his jeans on the floor. He heard the cell phone clunk as it fell from his pocket. Zanthe had only phoned once last night. Her voice had been younger than Doc had expected—the voice of a girl, shaken.

"I hope you're proud of yourself," she had said.

"Hell yes," he'd boomed then. But now, bending to pick the phone up, he wasn't so sure. Rubbing his back, he caught a glimpse of his naked self in the vanity mirror—red-faced, slack, full-bellied, furry. *I found myself in a dark woods, lost*, he thought.

"I'm an old fool," he said.

Sue said nothing, only folded the covers back and patted the pillow beside her, and after a minute Doc set the phone on the dresser and crawled into bed with his wife.

ONE OF US

KYLE CALLED HIS MOTHER Karen when she was being nice and Madam No when she wasn't, and it was my job to talk to her when she wasn't. Usually she was mad at Noah, Kyle's older brother, but tonight when she phoned she was mad at his girlfriend.

"What's her name?" I asked.

"Angina Pectoris," Karen snapped.

That's an odd name, I thought, but did not say. I have walked into Karen's traps before. "What's she like?" I asked instead. I kept my voice down so as not to disturb Kyle, who was writing a paper for his law professor and watching the game on the couch with the sound turned off.

"Let's just say she's perfect." I heard Karen light a cigarette and I held the phone at arm's length. Second hand smoke couldn't zoom from her house in Memphis all the way to our apartment in San Diego—I knew that—but I was only seven weeks along and taking no chances. "A perfect twenty-eight year old twice-divorced born-again unemployed dog walker who lives in a trailer, rides a Harley, and has a six-year-old daughter named Neavaeh, which you should know is Heaven misspelled backward." I heard my father-in-law giggle in the background. Men don't usually giggle but I can't imagine Leif laughing any other way.

"She must be pretty if Noah likes her," I fished.

"Noah's an idiot." I waited for Karen to say, *Why oh why can't my sons find women worthy of them*—which was exactly what she had said two years ago when she first met me—but she smoked in silence. I waited. I was glad about the little girl—Noah loved kids—and I was glad his girlfriend was a dog walker. Karen and Leif had both said about ten million times how sorry they were that I worked in a dentist's office. I was not surprised when Karen said, "They're getting married next month," but I was surprised when she added, "And if that's not bad enough she's an orphan."

An orphan? I pressed a hand to my stomach. "That's terrible. What happened to her parents?"

"Who knows? What happened to yours?"

Sometimes the only way to handle Karen is to hang up. I did, and finished making Kyle's dinner while I waited for her to phone back. I hadn't touched red meat, sugar, or wine since I found out about the baby, but Kyle liked spaghetti the way Karen and Leif made it and I'd been trying to perfect the recipe they gave me, even though I'm pretty sure they left something out.

"We were cut off," Karen said when she called back. "Look, April, no doubt your parents are stellar people. But they didn't pay a cent for your wedding. We did. And now it seems we have to pay for Noah's wedding too." Her voice broke. She was crying. "I'm sure you can see our point. It's just not fair." She blew her nose. "Is Kyle there?"

Kyle raised his fists and jumped into the air as the Spurs went into overtime. "He's studying," I said.

After dinner Kyle made room on the couch and I curled up beside him and leafed through the wedding album on the coffee table. I know it's bad to brag, but Kyle and I had the best wedding of anyone we know. All his fraternity brothers were there and a lot of his ex-girlfriends, at least the ones I knew about. I wore Karen's old wedding dress and my skin was perfect for once. At the reception we danced to "In Your Eyes" and the next day we went to Cabo. It was the happiest day of my life and it wasn't my fault my parents couldn't afford to come. Leif and Karen were all smiles in their matching navy blue outfits that day, and Kyle stood so straight in his tux and Phi Beta Kappa pin, and I was practically hidden behind that huge bouquet of daisies Noah had picked for me. For the first time I noticed Noah wasn't in any of the family pictures, though there was one of him dancing barefoot on the lawn with a caterer and another of him sneaking a finger-full of frosting off the cake, smiling so hard he looked electrified. I smiled back; I love Kyle's big brother even though he can get pretty wild sometimes. I closed the album. "I hope Noah and his new wife will be as happy as we are," I said.

Kyle kissed the top of my head. "Noah's always been happy," he said. "That's his problem."

Karen and Leif met us at the airport when we flew in for Noah's wedding. They were dressed alike, in matching polo shirts and copper bracelets and khaki shorts and clip on sunglasses. Holding hands as they led the way to the car, they looked like paper doll cut-outs: sweet. I always wanted them to sound as sweet as they looked, and I was never ready for what Kyle called their "sense of humor."

Leif started: "The love birds had us to dinner last night . . ." He giggled as he started the car. "You should see her trailer."

"Whore décor." Karen turned around in the seat to grin at us. "Shags, shams, leopard-skin chandeliers. Not a single bookcase."

I grinned back. I could not imagine a leopard-skin chandelier but at least Kyle and I had a bookcase.

"And guess what she served?" Leif began.

"Steak!" Karen finished. "Champagne and wild rice with truffles and strawberry pie from the most expensive bakery in town."

My stomach lurched. "Yum."

"Not 'yum.' Dumb. You know what she has in her refrigerator?"

I punched Kyle's knee but he was staring out the window. Kyle always found plenty in his own head to occupy him.

"Butter. Real butter. This while Noah is out in the hot sun, working construction . . ."

"*De*-struction," Leif corrected, ". . . and she's hardly working at all. Yet she buys real butter."

I had to agree that was extravagant. One thing Karen and I had in common was thrift. We are both penny pinchers. We stopped at the market on the way to their house and pulled out our coupons. Karen thumped watermelons while I sorted green beans. "Oops," I said, pulling one bad bean from the bag, "I should of looked better."

Karen stopped in the aisle and stared at me. "What?" Other shoppers turned to stare too.

"I should *have* looked . . ." I said.

A girl about my age rolled her eyes as she passed with her cart but to tell the truth, I didn't mind when Karen corrected me. There was (were?) lots I needed to learn. Kyle had a brilliant law career ahead of him, everybody said so, and I didn't want to do anything, ever, to embarrass him in public. I was glad when Karen turned back to the melons and I was glad, too, we hadn't told her and Leif about the baby yet. They had grilled me after I lost the last one: was I doing too much at the gym, had I been drinking, had I been working too late at the clinic, et cetera, and I wasn't going to go through that again. I would be three months along on Noah's wedding day, and that's when Kyle was going to make the announcement.

"Good to be home?" Leif asked me as we pulled into traffic again. I nodded, even though Tennessee is not my home. My dad's military and I grew up in Kentucky, Georgia, California, North Carolina, Puerto Rico, and Hawaii. I leaned against Kyle in the back seat and looked out at the cars shimmering past us in the heat.

"Rolling stone," Karen said, smiling at me over her shoulder. She turned back to Leif. "Until she took one look at our little Kyle and started rolling after him. Stalked him all through school, didn't she. Oh well." She yawned. "How else was she going to get him?" Quietly, in the back seat, Kyle pressed my hand. He was shaking.

I forget sometimes that it's hard for him too, being around them. Noah was parked outside their house in his truck. "Idiot," Karen shouted at him. "It's over one hundred degrees! Why didn't you wait inside?"

"Your door's locked." Noah looked like the friendly giant from a picture book with his shaggy orange hair and big grin and when he picked me up for a hug I had to warn him "Careful!" which made him the first to know about the baby, and when I whispered "Don't tell," he just smiled and set me down gentle as gentle. His girlfriend didn't smile when she got out of the truck but she shook hands. She was a tall blonde with a slight malocclusion but a great figure. Neavaeh was just plain adorable. She wanted to sit on the couch with me and show me her scrapbook, which was like my wedding album, only full of drawings of Hannah Montana. Karen and Leif disappeared into the kitchen—they never let anyone help them cook—and Noah and Kyle went outside to look at some problem with Noah's truck, and Angina just sat very straight on a chair by the front door like she was already ready to leave.

I asked to see her ring, which was bigger than mine but not as nice, and I asked about her wedding dress, which Karen had already warned me cost one thousand dollars, and I admired her French manicure and did not tell her what those fumes could do to an embryo, nor, though I wanted to, did I ask what it had been like growing up in an orphanage. I wanted to say *welcome to the family and I hope we'll be sisters* but I thought she'd probably just stare at me like I was crazy so I looked around the living room for something else to talk about. Leif and Karen are famous entomologists and the coffee table was covered with their bug books, but I didn't know what to say about those, and the mantel had so few photos of Noah and so many photos of Kyle that I thought I'd better not say anything about those either. So instead I talked about how I'd met Kyle—cleaning his teeth!—and how I'd had to steady him because he was shaking so hard when the dentist came in to do his filling. Angina sat still and listened but didn't say anything herself, and I guessed she'd met Noah in a bar, and I decided to shut up.

I was relieved when Leif rang the cowbell and we all sat down to dinner. "I hope you don't mind leftovers," Karen said. "With all the wedding expenses, we can't afford steak and strawberries." I ducked my head at that, but Noah said, "Oh boy, am I ever starving!" and began to pass the platters of ham and potato salad. I watched him down an entire glass of iced tea, barely swallowing, and I saw Neavaeh watching too; we smiled at each other. Setting his glass down, Noah said, "We ordered the flowers today."

"What?" Karen's dangerous *what.* "What did you get?"

"Regina's favorite," Noah smiled. "Orchids."

Regina? Oh. Okay.

"And what did you use for payment, pray?"

"We have your credit card number, remember?" Noah said.

I set my fork down. "What color are they?" I asked in the silence.

"Pink and white," Neaveah whispered. She pushed a piece of ham close to a clump of potato salad, touched my arm, and pointed. *See? Pink and white!* I tried to smile but could not.

"Take them back," Karen said.

"Fine." Noah shrugged.

"We can't," Regina said quietly. "Remember?"

"Jesus H. Christ," Karen spat.

I glanced at Leif. If my mother ever swore at the table my father would bust her face open. But Leif went on eating. Karen lit a cigarette and I looked at Kyle, who nodded, so I said, "Excuse me" and went to his old bedroom, where I curled on the bunk bed holding my stomach and wondering how we were all going to get through the next two days until the wedding.

Somehow we did. Leif and Karen's barks were worse than their bites—Kyle had always told me that—especially if you looked at what they did and didn't listen to what they said. Still, they were definitely different from any people I had ever met before. They knew about a zillion different facts about a zillion different things and around the house they talked to each other in Latin. Kyle could understand it but I was just as happy to let the sounds roll off of me. I didn't want to know how upset they were about the two wedding cakes when they'd only offered to pay for one, or the expensive pastor who had his own television show, or the ridiculous country club Regina wanted for her ridiculous reception. Karen usually had a string of wet dental floss dangling out of her mouth even when she went to the store and Leif padded around the house barefoot in a sarong with a magnet headband for his migraines. In the mornings Karen did aerobics and Leif did yoga and then they sat together in the backyard side by side and smoked cigarettes. In the afternoons they went to their swim club—they liked swimming, Kyle said, because it was the only sport that let them hit, kick, and spit at the same time. It was strange how sharp Kyle got when he was around his parents. He'd brought his law books along and while he was studying, I'd either nap or make lists of baby names or drive around with Noah and Neavaeh as they did last minute errands for the wedding.

The morning of the wedding was hot again, one hundred and two before noon. I dressed in the same suit I wore on our honeymoon, which luckily still fit with the skirt unbuttoned in back, and tried to do something with my skin, which had gone ballistic. I wasn't coloring my hair anymore and I'd been expecting Karen to say something but she didn't seem to notice I was brown now. Leif didn't either. This was odd, because the whole family had a thing about redheads. "You must be one of us," Kyle had said, the first time he met me. I didn't have any idea what he was talking about, but when I met his family later, and saw how they looked alike, I knew I fit right in. None of us had eyebrows or eyelashes and all of us burned like crazy in the sun. I liked being a redhead but after Oprah said that the chemicals in hair dye could get into your blood stream and hurt your baby, I'd thrown my Clairol away. Now my hair was the same color as Neavaeh's, and probably, I thought, the same color as Regina's, if she'd let it grow out.

Leif and Kyle looked handsome in their tuxedos but it took a minute to get used to Karen's outfit. She was in a bright pink sheath with white polka dots and a floppy pink hat with a huge white feather. "You like?" She pirouetted in front of us. "I found it at the Salvation Army. Thirty-nine dollars. With everything else we're paying for I didn't see how I could afford another mother-of-the-groom outfit."

I remembered the navy blue she'd worn to our wedding and wondered where it was, but I didn't say anything. None of us did, except Leif who said, "Don't worry, I brought two," when Karen cried, "Oh god I forgot my tongue scraper."

We drove in silence to the church. I tried to stay awake but could not and when I woke up we were parked in some field under an enormous white cross. The church was big and new and empty and when Karen found out there was no air conditioning, she lost it. She started storming around in her pink shoes looking for someone in charge but all the offices were empty and we couldn't find a thermostat. "Idiots," Karen kept saying, about Noah and Regina, "stupid, stupid idiots." She threw herself down into a pew with her arms crossed and closed her eyes.

She may have kept them closed through the whole ceremony; I was too hot myself to notice much. I felt bad that there were so few people on the bride's side of the aisle—only three of Regina's girlfriends and her boss from the dog-walking place. A friend of her dead father's gave her away. With his little white beard he looked like my Uncle Mitch and for a moment I missed my mother and father with all my heart. They hadn't always been there for me, but blood is blood and I promised myself that I would phone them as soon as Kyle made the announcement about the baby.

After I decided that, I sat up straighter and tried to focus on the ceremony. Weddings make me want to re-marry Kyle, and the things the pastor was saying about being each other's best friend and supporting your partner no matter what are things I believe in. Noah looked happy and handsome and Regina really did look radiant, though she had to keep blowing her bangs up it was so hot and there were flies in the church that kept landing on her veil. Her dress wasn't worth a thousand dollars—it didn't even have a train that bustled up. Still, she was a beautiful bride, and when she and Noah kissed, I did what I always do at weddings, and cried. Kyle pulled a handkerchief out of his tuxedo and handed it to me with a little bow as he passed on the aisle.

Then it was wait wait wait while the photographer took pictures and then it was drive drive drive while we tried to find the country club. It was called Rolling Hills—"Rolling Heels," Leif giggled, but we were all too tired to giggle with him, and Karen wasn't talking at all. I hoped I could sit with Kyle at the table with the Reserved sign, but they'd put me somewhere else, so I had to sit with some university friends of Karen and Leif. I sent my chicken back, because it had wine sauce, but the nice waiter brought me extra white rice and salad and I did my best to pay attention to the others talking about old times. On the second or third round of champagne, someone said something about Noah, how well he'd turned out, "considering."

I perked up. "Considering what?" I asked and the wife of one of the friends put down her glass and said, "Well how he was born," and I said, "How *was* he born?" and her husband nudged her but she said, "You know. In a cave. When Karen and Leif were grad students and high as kites on acid." She had to stop because her husband took her glass away. My jaw dropped and I turned to look at Karen in her big hat and Leif, both of them sitting calmly at the head table, as if they had never been anything but perfect, and then I swiveled to stare at Kyle who had just stepped up to the stage to give his best man speech. Did he know? I wondered. Did he know his brother Noah had been poisoned in the womb? I bet he did not.

"I'd like to propose a toast to my crazy brother and his unlucky bride," Kyle began, and his voice broke a little in the cute way it does and Noah beamed and Regina smiled, blowing her bangs up. I took a deep breath, remembering Noah's toast to us, when we got married, his brimming eyes as he called me an angel and Kyle his hero.

"Noah is the most dependable man I know—that is, you can always depend on him to do the wrong thing at the wrong time," Kyle said. People laughed. "Noah has broken every bone in his body, flunked out of every school, been thrown off every baseball team, basketball team, soccer team, and hockey team, all for different reasons but mostly for being uncoordinated, unreliable, and stoned. He's totaled six cars, two of them mine, run at least one lawnmower into a neighbor's swimming pool, been fired from more jobs than you can shake a stick at. In fact, one of the more recent jobs he was fired from *was* a job you shake a stick at: he was a baton twirler in a clown circus and even they didn't want him." People were laughing still but less easily now. Kyle stopped to adjust the orchid in his buttonhole and when I saw his hands were shaking I wanted to go up to him and say *Stop now honey*, but he went on: "Noah has been arrested for arson, vandalism, and loitering, and he has, at this very moment, four unpaid parking tickets, twenty useless lottery tickets, a box of condoms with holes in them, and a baggie of pot in the glove compartment of his truck. He kidnaps strays, any lost dog or cat that he sees on the street he just puts in his truck, spends hundreds fixing them up at the vets and then lets them loose on the street again. Once he accidentally ran over a dog he'd just rescued." Neavaeh gasped but Leif giggled and when I glanced over I saw that he and Karen were smiling up at Kyle, nodding like twins in synchronized approval. "He goes anywhere he's asked, loves to party, and is the kind of drinker who heads for a beer down the block and winds up in a hotel in Miami with only one shoe and no wallet. He owns nothing but the clothes on his back and his truck, which was paid for by my poor parents, whom he continues to rip off every chance he gets, present occasion not excepted."

I was too stunned to move. Noah was too. He sat with his lips parted, wanting to smile, but not able to. Regina, beside him, crouched like a tigress in her chair, eyes blazing.

"To conclude," Kyle said, "My brother Noah is a loser, pure and simple, always has been, always . . ."

Both Neavaeh and I shouted, "Watch out!" at the same time but we were too late because Regina had leapt on Kyle and knocked him down. Karen jumped up, scattering silver and crystal, and grabbed Regina's veil, Regina wheeled and slugged her, Leif screamed like a girl, Noah just stood there staring and I did something I never do and threw up in public.

The ride home was quiet. I'd brought a napkin and a glass of ice cubes with me and I made sure Kyle kept his head back so his nose would stop bleeding. "If she'd just let you finish your speech," Karen fumed. "Didn't she know you were going to end it by saying that because of meeting her, Noah had changed? That she'd made him a better man?"

"Oh, I think *she's* the better man," Leif said. He said something in Latin that made all three of them giggle.

I raised my voice. "Tell them about the baby, Kyle."

It was the first time I'd ever told Kyle what to do and I was too amazed at myself to even listen as he made the announcement. I was wondering what to tell my own parents. Usually my mom calls drunk and I let the machine take it. My dad's in the brig again, my brother weighs three-hundred pounds, and my sister practically lives in rehab.

But no one in my family has ever taken acid in a cave.

"In Your Eyes" came on the radio. I leaned forward. "Turn it up," I said. I took Kyle's free hand and placed it firmly on my belly. I could tell he didn't want to keep it there—he was shaking again—but I held on tight. No matter what, I was going to hold on tight.

GHOST DOG

I ALWAYS KNOW WHEN I'm being watched, it's one of the first things I learned growing up like I did. So when I heard the leaves rustle behind me and felt the air shift, I just acted dumb, kept my head down, and went on with my work. It was noon, already hot, the way it gets in Kaua'i when the trade winds drop, and I had almost finished the lily pond I was building for Les. I had cleared the bamboo and dredged the stream and had just begun the pretty part, lining it with coral. Whistling, I reached for the heaviest chunk I could find and wheeled around, ready to throw.

But there was no need. My stalker was old, starved, all bones and bristle, with eyes so white they had to be blind. Her back legs were stunted; the top of her head was flat; she might have been part wolf or hyena. Some of the millionaires and rock stars on the island kept illegal pets—tigers, apes, panthers, even snakes—and then they neglected them. This animal was probably an escapee, like me. I reached in my pocket for a piece of banana bread and crouched to offer it to her, but just then Simon began screaming from the guest house and his girlfriend Sonia started to giggle, like she does, as if she likes it, and the dog, or whatever it was, backed into the jungle and disappeared. I didn't blame her.

"Hey sweetheart!" Simon—flushed face, fat breasts spilling over the waistband of his boxers—stood on the balcony and bellowed down at me. "Have you forgotten that even sex fiends need to eat? Where's lunch?"

I wiped my hands on my shorts, put my tools away, and went up to the house, stopping at the garden first to pick some lettuce and sweet corn. I took a deep breath of the plants, inhaling the peppery basil and banana tree scents to steady myself. Simon and Sonia had been with us a week too long. Les didn't pay attention to their fights; he was either down at the building site or at his computer, but I'd been having a hard time ever since they arrived. I had to be polite, because Simon was backing Les on The Center, so I cooked and made their drinks and did their laundry—blood on the sheets where he hit her or she bit him, who could tell—but I didn't like to be around them. I grew up with drunks and they are not my favorite people.

Les came up from the site when Simon blew the conch shell and Sonia wandered down in her black bikini bottom and a Spanish shawl and we all sat outside by the waterfall, trying to ignore the helicopters flying overhead. Simon made fun of Les's steamed rice and green salad, but Les didn't care, he just laughed and pulled me onto his lap. Les had lost fifteen pounds since I'd started cooking for him; his cholesterol had dropped and his blood pressure was almost normal again. Even Simon had to admit he looked better than he had before he met me.

"Nothing like a personal trainer," Les said, patting my thigh, something he'd never do if Simon wasn't watching. I wiggled off his lap as soon as I could and pretended to study my Japanese lesson while Sonia sunned herself and Les and Simon talked about people they'd known and the deals they'd put together in the past. After a while I put my book down and listened. I loved learning new things about Les. Before I knew him, when he was young, Les had traveled all over the world. He'd lived with Tibetan monks, studied acupuncture in China, worked with a shaman in Peru. He and Simon had run a holistic health institute in Los Angeles and had held a sexual awakening seminar in Arizona. I was wondering what kind of "awakening" Simon could inspire when he saw my smile, stopped talking, and said, "Are you sure she's not CIA?"

Les laughed and looked at me. "Don't worry, I think the worst thing she's ever been is a Baptist." His voice dropped and his smile was so deep and private I began to blush. "She's a good girl."

"She is?" Simon raised his dark glasses to wink at me and I saw the new scratches on his face. "We'll have to do something about that."

After lunch Les and Simon went out to look at some property on the other side of the island in the Jeep. Sonia was my job; I was supposed to take her to the beach, if she wanted, or shopping, if she wanted, or just leave her alone. "What would you like to do?" I asked.

She was sipping tequila and painting her nails.

"I'm happy," she drawled, her voice flat.

I looked at her. Sonia was about thirty and gorgeous. Dark eyes, dark hair. She should have been happy. But she didn't take care of herself. She was overweight, with bruises everywhere. She had a tattoo of a dragon coiled around her navel and her skin smelled smoky and unclean. She hardly ever talked and when she did she was hard to hear, partly because of her accent, which was Brazilian, and partly because she was always stoned.

I picked up the bottle of dark red polish. My hands were pretty beat-up from garden work, but I had nice feet. "Do you mind?" I gestured toward my toenails.

Sonia shrugged and sipped her tequila. There was a new purple hickey on her throat. I thought of Simon's brown rabbit teeth and felt sick. "Can I ask you something?" she said, in her slow way. "Why are you with Les?"

Everyone asked that, I guess because of the age difference, and I never answered, because what was the point. But for some reason I wanted to tell Sonia the truth. I flushed again, remembering Les's warm eyes and the way his lips always tipped up when he smiled at me. I thought of his hard Buddha belly and the way his hair curled like baby goat horns all over his big brainy head. I thought of the home he had offered me here, the first home I had ever felt safe in. "I love him," I said.

Sonia lay back and fingered the fangs on her dragon as if they were real. After a while, she said, "And how did you meet him?"

Again I wanted to either say nothing, or, better, lie and tell her it had been romantic, that I'd saved Les from a shark attack or that he had waltzed me across a moonlit balcony, but, once more, I told the truth. Not the whole truth. Sonia didn't need to know that I had come to the islands with a church group. "I answered an ad. He needed a housekeeper."

She touched her full bottom lip with her finger while I studied my feet, which looked ridiculous. I opened the polish remover and took all the red off. "I'm going to the market," I said. "You can come if you like."

She didn't answer but by the time I walked out toward the car she was dressed and waiting. She slipped into the front seat and tied a scarf around her head. With her sunglasses and big red lips she looked like a cartoon of glamour and for once I was glad to be myself, thin and freckled as I am.

We climbed up the canyon, past all the gated plantations. Escaped pet parrots and macaws shrilled from the palm trees, and black and golden roosters foraged through the tall grass at the highway's edge. To make conversation, I told Sonia about the strange dog I'd seen that morning, but she wasn't interested. "It might have been a ghost," I said. She leaned her head back, eyes closed, bored. But I was excited. I remembered the dog's white eyes and way it had disappeared back into the jungle like smoke. "I've seen a lot of ghosts," I went on. "Once my mother told me the foster home was on fire and because of that I was able to get the other kids out in time and one night I talked to a boy at a shelter who had hung himself. Of course I've never seen an animal ghost before but that doesn't mean they don't exist. I mean if there's one thing Les has taught me, it's to trust what I see."

"Les taught you that?" she drawled, lifting her head.

"Well, yes. You know. Visualization. It's part of the philosophy of The Center."

Sonia smiled, lush and lazy, and I pulled into the market at Princeville. She had no cash of course so I bought her cigarettes and more tequila, but when she wasn't looking I slipped the gallon of ice cream she'd chosen back in the freezer and replaced the huge tin of salted macadamia nuts that she and Simon chewed like monkeys with a bag of organic almonds. She looked at magazines while I paid and said not a word on the drive back. Since she clearly didn't care, I decided to do something I'd been wanting to do anyway, so instead of heading straight home, I turned up toward the Japanese graveyard at the top of the hill, pulled over and stopped.

I admire the Japanese. Their gardens are the best in the world and even though this little graveyard hadn't been tended in years, there were orange amaryllis and flame trees everywhere and the moss and maple plantings were stunning. Some of the mounds actually had bonsai on them. Sonia stayed in the car, head against the seat, as I got out and sketched the headstones. Pitted, porous, cocoa-colored and specked with lichen—they were exactly what I wanted lining the path to the lily pond. I tried to read the inscriptions but my Japanese wasn't good enough yet and most of the characters had been worn away by weather. One polished plaque in English said "Iku Shimoda, Beloved Young Auntie" and that made me sad, for Iku Shimoda had been buried in a plot beside a married couple and I imagined she'd worked hard and never had anything of her own.

Before returning to the car, I stopped to take in the view—green valley, misty fluted mountains—it was the perfect place for The Center—or would be, as soon as Les got Simon's signature on the loan.

Les wanted to take us all out that night but Simon and Sonia had to have their drinks first and then their coke and then their pot and by the time we got to town the restaurants had closed and it took Les going into Poliahu's and talking to the owner to get us served. Simon was really loud by then and even Sonia had started to talk, or sing rather, some flitty little bossa nova tune that she thought was cute and kept humming under her breath. She insisted on karaoke and got up on the deserted stage and sang, "I Touch Myself," her eyes on Les the whole time. On the way home she leaned over the back seat and tugged at Les's earring with her teeth. Les gasped when she bit and I swung around to slap her but Les caught my hand. When I touched his ear there was blood on it. I was upset but there was nothing I could do.

When we got home there were more drinks and more coke. I kept zoning out but swallowed my yawns and made myself stay awake even though my ears were ringing and I was so tired I felt like I was curled inside a seashell. Les started talking to Sonia in some soft fast language and it took me a while to realize he was speaking in Portuguese. I couldn't understand the words but I knew he was talking about The Center and explaining to her, as he had explained to me, how the dynamics of charged visual energy could heal the sick and change people's lives. Teachers from India and Tibet were going to come and there would be a famous Zen chef and a resident drummer. I was going to do the garden—every sort of fruit, vegetable, and tropical flower, even a palm orchard.

Sonia listened with a half-smile while Les told her all this, then she got up and started to dance. Simon was slumped in a hammock by then but I could see Les watching her. His lips were curved up and his eyes had that focused look that meant he was thinking, hard.

I didn't like it.

Les and I had never fought and we did not fight that night. We lay in bed like we always did, with our arms around each other. "How much longer are they going to be here?" I asked.

"I don't know," he said. "There aren't any signatures yet. It's complicated."

He sounded sad. I rolled toward him and kissed his worry spot—he had this triangular wrinkly pouch between his eyes—and then I kissed all over his neck and shoulders then slowly kissed low, lower, the way he liked, but he pulled my face up and rolled away. After he dropped off, I tried to focus on my breathing but I couldn't get centered. I tried to think about the lily pond, the way it would look when it was finished,and how pleased Les would be, sitting out there with his students, and me, in the mornings.

I heard a noise outside the window and sat up. When I slipped out to the veranda I saw the ghost dog below, her eyes like pearls in the moonlight. I tiptoed down the stairs to find some food to set out for her but who was in the kitchen but Simon, standing in his swim shorts rummaging through the freezer looking for his stupid ice cream.

"I forgot to buy it," I said.

"It wasn't your responsibility. It was Sonia's. I asked her specifically to do this one thing for me."

"Guess she forgot."

"I'll have to settle for this crap." He tore open the bag of almonds. I shrugged and sat down at the table.

"I can't sleep," I said. "What's good for when you can't sleep?"

"Ice cream, sweetheart. Why do you think I want it?" He slumped down beside me, fat thighs so close I had to force myself not to move back.

"Les is the amazing one," I chattered. "He can sleep no matter what. Even when he's worried. And I know he's worried." I paused and looked up at Simon as steadily as I dared. "He doesn't think you're going to go in with him on The Center."

Simon shrugged and crunched a handful of almonds. He and Les had met in Mexico thirty-five years ago. I'd always wanted to ask him about Les's other women, the three ex-wives and all the girl friends who came before me, but there was something about Simon that told me he never knew any of those women well enough to tell me anything I'd want to know. Or maybe I was just afraid of what he'd say. "It's not up to me," he said at last. "It's Sonia."

"What does she have to do with it?"

"Have you never heard of a cash cow?"

I blinked. Sonia was the one with the money?

"Sonia," Simon said, "is not very spiritual, as you may have noticed. She is not into meditation or whatever fucking scam Les plans to run here."

"It's not a scam," I flared, "it's a sacred and very ancient Chakra technique—"

But Simon shushed me. "Blah blah," Simon said. "Let's face it, sweetheart. Les has had a lot of irons in a lot of fires over a lot of years. He's had enough fake business cards to build a paper shithouse."

I was silent. I knew Les had tried many different avenues. But they had all been leading here. To The Center. To us.

"Sonia," Simon said, "believes in the life of the body. She likes pleasure. She also likes pain. You know?"

"Yeah. Everyone on the island knows. She's loud enough."

"The person who is freaking this deal," Simon said, "is you."

"What do you mean?"

He looked at me steadily.

"Look," I blurted, "I don't care if he sleeps with her."

Simon laughed.

"It's just sex."

He lit a cigarette, blew the smoke in my face.

I dropped my eyes. He was right. I wouldn't be able to stand it. And if I couldn't stand it Les wouldn't do it and if Les didn't do it he'd lose The Center.

I looked up at Simon, who nodded. "Good girl," he said.

So this meant what it had always meant: it meant I'd have to leave. I'd always had to leave.

Simon touched the top of my head as he rose. "Good girl," he repeated.

It sounded like a curse.

I looked around the kitchen, at the shelves filled with jars of baby corn and okra and mango jam I'd put up, at the stalks of red ginger in the tall vases, at the photos of Les and me at the beach and hiking up the volcano, at the plans for The Center I'd colored and framed and hung on the walls. The Center was going to be a lot different with Sonia's money. It would probably have a piercing parlor and a karaoke room.

My backpack still hung on the hook where I'd left it a year ago, the day I hiked in from Lihue to answer the ad. I looked inside—my Bible was still there, my broken sandals, my old Swiss Army knife. I picked it up and headed toward the door. I got as far as the lily pond before I turned back. I could see the guesthouse lit up and Sonia's fat shape beginning to sleepwalk across the catwalk toward our bedroom, mine and Les's. *Maybe he won't open the door,* I thought. It had started to rain like it does in Kaua'i at night, just a rush in the dark like doves' wings, and I crouched under the mango tree in my white nightgown and prayed like I hadn't prayed since I left the mainland. Something slithered behind me and I jumped, but it was only the dog, come back. I couldn't see her and when I put my hand out I couldn't feel her, but I knew she was there. I could hear her breathing and I was not afraid. I'd been alone in the dark before, and I'd had worse companions. When Les opened the door and let Sonia in, I stood up and made my way toward the highway, the dog lagging a heartbeat behind me. When the surfer boys stopped at dawn, I got in their car. I did not look back. Not because I was brave—I've never been brave—but because I wasn't ready to admit that nothing was there.

A TALE OF CALAMITY

BLUE EYES, FLYAWAY HAIR, SNAGGLE TEETH, smile like a young boy's, thin fingers plucking the sleeve of my jumper, that was Rita—lovely, loopy Rita. She'd been widowed since August and had no one but me. When she heard her two older sisters were coming to the island, one from the States, one from Australia, she ran down the hill to my shop in the rain. *Annie, Annie, what shall I do? What shall I feed them? What shall I wear?* She hadn't seen either of the sisters in twenty years. Some trouble over money, she said, some kink in the will when their father died, or maybe (though she did not say so) some disapproval of Joe. *What if they hate it here?* She bummed one of my American cigarettes and paced around the shop shivering and barefoot, her muddy boots propped by my door. *What if they want to take me away?*

So I rang up Eileen and Eileen rang Young Edna, and we four worked like donkeys getting Rita's house ready. We threaded crêpe paper streamers through the rafters and polished the windows and the tall hall mirror and set Joe's poetry books out for display. The morning of the sisters' arrival, Eileen filled jars with yellow roses and Young Edna set out wine and glasses, and I put a roast in Rita's cooker and left my lemon cake to cool on her counter. We were all fairly knackered and looked it, but there we were anyway, down at the pier at noon when the whistle sounded and the boat came in from Cleggan.

It was a fine day, green and silver, one of those island days when even the gulls sound tuneful. I had a shopping cart for the sisters' luggage and Rita jiggled the handle like a child while Eileen and Young Edna, who *were* children, snapped their fingers and stepped around to music on their iPods only they could hear.

Some Germans got off the ferry first and then four tall Danes with their bicycles and then a group of school children from Connemara and then *he* pushed through. I should have seen him for a devil at once, but in my defense my glasses were new and giving me grief. All I remember is a young man with a brown beard and a red scarf, the only hint of dementia being the way he headed straight for the pub as if drink was the one reason he'd come to the island, and maybe it was; they say he stayed at The Currach until Colm threw him out, and after he smashed the church altar he went up to Donal's until Jack evicted him at midnight.

The sisters were last to come down the ramp, Rosemary and Regina. There was no mistaking them, they looked like Rita, with their blue eyes and pink cheeks, and to their credit they did not hold back. The very minute they saw her they lifted their arms and for the next five minutes it was hugs and kisses, tears and laughter. I had to wipe my own eyes when Rita introduced me: "This is Annie, who saved my life after Joe died," and though this was not true and I said so, it made me flush with pride nonetheless. Eileen and Young Edna shook hands politely and then darted after the Danes—those girls were wild and no one expected them to last the summer and in fact they did not.

Rosemary, the American, said, "Thank you Annie; we hated thinking of Rita all alone out here," and Regina, the Australian, said, "She's our baby, you know," but in a gentle way that sounded well-intended and there was more laughter as we set back up the hill. The sisters asked a hundred questions; they wanted to know about the seabirds and the sheep and the youth hostel and especially about my craft shop, so we stopped there on the way up. They could not get enough of Whimsy, curled on the window box among the geraniums, and they petted old Gypsy, sleeping under the counter. Rosemary said, "Look at all your quaint little things! I can't help it, I'm a shopper," and went on to prove it by buying an Aran sweater from China (I did not tell her China) for her grandson and a knit cap for herself and though I hesitated I charged her no less than I would charge any tourist and took her money as I would anyone's. Regina just moved around the shop smiling to herself and picking up jars of jam and honey and looking on the bottom before setting them down. It was she who noticed my certificates of completion on the wall and congratulated me for taking so many postal courses. "Joe always said if

Annie had gone to regular university she would be a professor by now," Rita boasted, coming up beside me. "He said she knew everything."

"Only unimportant things," I corrected her.

"Saving Rita's life after Joe died," Regina said, "was not unimportant."

"Ah, she was easy to save. I just fed her," I protested.

"Fed me and listened to me," Rita added. "Let me weep and wail on her shoulder all hours of the day and night."

"You see?" I said. "No genius needed."

We continued up the hill and talking all the time the sisters admired Rita's view, Rita's garden, the low stone steps to Rita's front door. I frankly thought they were overdoing it, but then I have never known how families behave. My husband died young, we had no children; my brothers disappeared long ago. I keep myself busy but there's a lack in my life; I don't deny it and I would not have minded having two sisters who looked like me arrive at long last to praise my way of living.

Rita's rooms gleamed when she opened the door and the sisters said "Ah!" and I could see all three blue-eyed faces shining in the tall hall mirror. The sunlight was coming in through the windows, turning the crêpe streamers pink and gold and the roast lamb and roses and lemon cake scented the air. Rita had the photograph album of the three sisters as children out on the table along with the Spanish wine and Joe's books and the newspaper clippings about Joe's death. The sisters sat down to catch up on their old lives so I left and said I'd see them tomorrow, but of course I never did.

I went back to the shop. I was humming a bit under my breath because Rita looked so radiant and I was happy for her, after her long winter of missing Joe. The shop was busy that day. I sold some honey to a German doctor and some of the beaded earrings I make from a kit to three schoolgirls. A studious American couple who had been on the island for a week came in and the wife said she had seen a white cow rise from the mist in the old graveyard that morning.

"Isn't that a sign that something bad is going to happen on the island?" the wife wanted to know. "I read in our guide book that whenever the white cow appears someone dies."

Usually I go along with this because it's good for business, but I was still feeling the glow from Rita and her sisters and I shook my head. "It's a sign that Frankie Ryan needs to put a new gate on his field," I said. "That eejit cow gets out all the time and tramples through Dory Conlin's vegetables and then there's solicitors you would not believe. Dory and Frankie have been at it for years."

The husband laughed but the wife looked disappointed. "What's the story about the big marble cross on the point, then?" she sulked.

"Sure, it was consecrated," I said, watching her relief as I began piling the brogue on, "for the two young lads who went swimming that day. They got as far as the wild rocks and t'was there," I paused to point the way the tourists enjoy, "the tide took 'em. T'was t'ree long days ere their poor dead bodies was recovered."

"Swimming!" the wife said, breathless, turning to her husband, "Imagine swimming around here! It's freezing! Who would ever swim in such cold water?"

I, who swim for a quarter hour every morning, rain or shine, shrugged and watched the two of them make their way down the hill, the husband holding his wife's elbow, both of them treading as carefully as if their young bones were glass. I remembered Rita, last winter, after Joe died, how when she left my shop for the village she'd edge down half the grassy path and then run and catch herself with an elbow around the gate post. Every day I'd think, *That's how she'll go; she'll fall and break her neck*, but I was wrong.

The day went on, a lovely day, the sheep going *Naaaa Naaaa* and the gulls squabbling and the waves smooth and green and the wildflowers waving yellow and purple on the cliffs. I heard the ferry whistle as it made the last run of the afternoon, no one but the schoolchildren on it. The Danes were cycling through the ruined abbey, the Americans were out looking for leprechauns, and the young man in the red scarf? Where was he? He was down at the The Currach drinking pint after pint; it was said he had thirteen pints by the time Colm threw him out, and his talk getting crazier by the minute.

"It was the usual drill," Colm said later. "Aliens. How aliens was infiltrating the stratosphere and getting into the ecosystem and taking over and had to be stopped. Dull gab. I often wish," Colm began, scratching his bald spot, "that madness had a bit more originality to it, y'know, more method," and then he stopped, because of what happened.

It was already starting, the madness, though I had no knowledge of it, and I closed the shop and went to the back, where I live, Whimsy and Gypsy following me in. I heated some soup and microwaved an apple tart and settled down to my assignment in Creative Fiction. I have completed twenty postal courses these last ten years. I have received high marks in Italian, String Theory, The History of the Ottoman Empire, and Lapidary Science. My instructions that day said to write "A 500 Word Description of a Place You'd Like to Visit" and I couldn't think of one because I like it here on Bofin, and see no need to leave, so I just sat staring out the window at the sea with my pen in my hand and my tea cooling beside me and finally began to write about the Taj Mahal, as a way to please my instructor.

As for the sisters, for them I hope it was laughter and lemon cake as they sat together on the couch and recounted the years that had taken one to America and one to Australia and left one stranded here. Not that Rita ever felt stranded, it had been she and Joe, after all, who erected the marble cross for the poor drowned boys. Maybe being sisters (but how should I know?) there were also quarrels and digs and reminders of past insults and injuries; maybe there was talk of the father and his will and why it no longer mattered that he'd left all to Rita; maybe all was forgiven, or not. In any event, at midnight they went to bed, and so, down the hill, did I.

Did no one hear the young man raving out by the rocks?

Did no one hear the young man climb the hill?

Did no one hear the young man pause at my door?

Did no one hear him pass on?

I believe I did not. I say I did not. I hope I did not. I pray I did not. But how to explain Whimsy batting my nose, trying to wake me, or Gypsy's low growl at the foot of my bed? How to explain the light through my window? Low and flickering, the light through my window.

Sometimes I dream of that light. I had seen it so often, all through the past winter, Rita moving with a candle through her house after midnight, weeping for Joe, afraid for herself, calling for me. Perhaps, that last night, when I shushed Whimsy, threw a pillow at Gypsy, and put my head under the blankets, I wanted no more. No more of Rita's tears and poor-me's and her what-will-I-do's? She had her sisters for that now. I wanted peace.

The young man, too, wanted peace. There was a roar in his ears and an engine where his heart should be and his mind was torn by ten thousand terrors. He could not remember Young Edna laughing at him as Eileen drew her away, whispering, "Can't you see he's a looney?" He did not remember the men pushing him toward Donal's door or the firm thrust of Jack's foot in the small of his back. He did not remember screaming in the dark church or wrestling the cross down and toppling the altar. All he remembered were aliens coming to get him and all he knew was that he had to hide. He could not hide at my house so he hid at Rita's. He went up her five stone steps and pushed against her unlocked front door and stepped into her dark living room smelling like lemons and women and roses and flicked his Zippo open and what the gardai say is that he must have seen his own white face in the hall mirror and it must have appalled him, it must have looked like an alien's face. He must have known he was not safe there either, so he lifted his lighter to the crêpe paper streamers and set the house on fire. When the three women came stumbling out through the smoke in their white nightgowns he screamed and fled. He did not stay to watch them crumple and burn, their charred bones not found until after the flames finally settled—for we have no firehouse on the island—huddled with their arms around each other near the front door. They'd made it that far and no farther.

There have been tragedies on the island before, shipwrecks and famines and drownings, but nothing like this, three innocent women. The tourists who come to see the abbey and the marble cross and Cromwell's castle now often look at the ruins of Rita's house as well and then they come into my shop to talk to me about it. I tell them what I know. I tell them how I miss her. I remember how Rita came every day last winter and I'd give her a sweet or a bit of chocolate because I knew how hard it is to live alone with nothing but the news on the radio, and how one day I had nothing but some raisins and she sucked each one as if they were precious figs from Persia and then said, "Thank you, Annie, you know what I need," and then the silly dangerous slipslide way she went down the grassy hill that made me laugh and made me worry too.

To keep from worry now, I've been working the latest assignment in my postal course. "Write a Tale of Calamity," the instructions say, and under Suggestions they list Losing Your Wallet, A Broken Bone, Death of a Pet. I keep thinking of that young man, how he threw himself into the harbor after, whether to drown or escape or try to swim back to Cleggan, who knows. The tide was out and only came up to his knees and he thrashed around, shouting "Help me! Help me!" almost comical, easy to capture, and Colm kept him locked in the pub's van until the gardai came by helicopter the next day, and he is in prison now, a young man, not yet thirty, sentenced for forty-eight years.

I think about that and put down my pen. This may be the first course I'm not able to finish.

ALICE CLAIMS HER INHERITANCE

ALICE GREW UP BELIEVING HER FATHER was a Scottish lord who died in the Highlands, shot through the heart in a freak hunting accident. No one knew where she got this idea. It might have been some story Josie told her during one of her blackouts but since it was a good story, and kept Alice quiet, no one saw fit to change it. Alice had no photos of her father, but she did have one of his books, a battered tennis handbook she'd found in a box with his name written in green ink on the inside cover: *B. Sinclair*, which was her name as well. Sinclair meant "pure, renowned, illustrious," words she looked up. Her mother Josie, stepfather Ern, and small half-brothers were all Grubbs. Grubbs was a German name that meant "mine workers." Dirty, smelly mine workers. *B. Sinclair* had never worked a mine in his life, Alice was sure of that, though he might have owned a few: gold mines, crystal mines, perhaps even emerald mines. He might even have owned a castle.

Josie's romance novels, which littered the trailer, often had castles on their covers, and though none of them were Scottish castles, exactly, Alice studied them. She could find no resemblance between the full-bosomed women on these covers and her short, fat, bespectacled mother, but she could see traces of herself in the handsome men embracing these women. The men had dark wavy hair, like hers, and straight slim bodies. Her father had surely been rich, intelligent, educated, and handsome. But why had he embraced someone like Josie? And what stupid thing had Josie done to alienate him and drag his daughter here, to the edge of the California desert, to live in a trailer filled with Grubbs?

"What are you sulking about now, princess?" Josie set down the laundry basket and threw a diaper at Alice, which Alice neatly deflected, never taking her stare off her mother as the diaper fell to the floor.

"I was just wondering," Alice said in her precise voice, "when I might claim my rightful inheritance?"

Josie had a big sloppy laugh. She pushed her glasses back up her nose and shook out another diaper. "Fancy words for a nine-year-old," she said approvingly. "Tell you what, Allie Cat, when you are twenty-one you can claim anything you want." She laughed again. "I did."

Alice stared at her mother—her frizzy hair, shapeless sweat pants, dirty feet in rubber thongs—and nudged the wheel of the stroller she was pushing back and forth to keep Little Lloyd from crying. One of the pit bull puppies came up and licked her ankle and she kicked it away. She felt like crying herself. Eleven years was a long time to wait for a castle, a crown, a title and lands. "So I don't get anything until I'm grown up?"

"You get to live your life," Josie said. She fingered the tarnished silver locket she always wore around her neck and studied Alice for a long moment before lighting a cigarette and exhaling. "What more d'ya want? Eggs in your beer?"

Josie often made no sense so Alice didn't bother to point out the obvious—that she never ate eggs and wouldn't touch a beer if she were paid to. Disgusted, she wheeled Little Lloyd out of the kitchen, past the television where Jip and Bobby wrestled in front of cartoons, past the boys' cluttered room, past the darkened bedroom where Ern, home from two weeks on the road as a trucker, slept, hands folded on top of his uniform, past the locked door of her own immaculate room (stopping to touch the key in her pocket to make sure it was still there), and back into the kitchen again.

"You're a liar," she announced unnecessarily, for Josie surely knew that at least about herself, "and I am going to Scotland to claim my rights as soon as I can afford a plane ticket."

"Good luck, kid," Josie said. "Drop me a line and let me know what you find out when you get there."

Alice did not find out anything for the next three years. She continued to survive as best she could in the foreignness of her family. She went to school early and came back late; she made friends but never invited them over, making sure her vacations were spent either at their homes or locked inside her spotless green and white bedroom with its ruffled curtains and canopied bed, while she practiced her handwriting until she had her father's *B* (for Balfour? Broderick? Baird?) *Sinclair* down perfectly. On the nights Ern was on the road and Josie was either at an AA meeting or a bar, Alice made oatmeal and scones for the boys. After she taught herself to sew, she made a fringed skirt in the red Sinclair plaid. She stayed coolly aloof unless crossed, at which time she threw such impressive tantrums that the Grubbs ceased to cross her. She came and went, ate and slept, as she pleased. She liked cleaning at night, creating some order out of the chaos of her mother's housekeeping. Sometimes she woke one of the boys and got him to help her bundle up the newspapers, wipe down the counters, empty the ashtrays, wash and dry the dishes. The Scots were a tidy people. The Scots were a thrifty people. She saved every cent she made doing odd jobs for neighbors and stashed the money in an empty tennis ball can she had wrapped in plaid gift paper. She came home one afternoon to find the tennis ball can empty and Josie passed out on the couch, surrounded by empty beer cans.

Alice threw such a spectacular tantrum over this that her Uncle Joe was called in to calm her. Uncle Joe was Josie's twin, the one, Josie said cheerfully, who'd had all the breaks, all the looks, all the money. He was a dentist now, a bachelor who lived with another bachelor in a city apartment. He sat down with Alice while she explained, rigid and calm, that she could not endure another day with her slatternly alcoholic, chain-smoking, lying, stealing whore of a mother. Uncle Joe closed his eyes in pain and shook his head. "Why are you so hard?" he sighed, and he pointed out the sacrifices Josie had made, letting her have her own room in the tiny trailer, scrimping to give her singing and tennis lessons, buying her new shoes and outfits every season while the boys lived in hand-me-downs. Alice stared at him, unrelenting. "I want to live with the Sinclairs," she said, "in Scotland."

"Out of the question," Uncle Joe said. Evading Alice's stare, he added, "Anyway, they moved."

"Where can I find them?" Alice persisted. "They are my real family and I should be living with them. Just because my father was shot through the heart—"

"Oh Christ," Uncle Joe interrupted. He sounded impatient. "Look." He gestured out the window where Josie, cigarette in mouth, hung sheets on a clothesline while Ern fiddled with the same motorcycle engine he'd been fiddling with since Christmas and the pit bulls rolled in the dirt and the three little boys threw rocks at each other. "This is your real family."

Alice screamed. Finally, as compromise, Uncle Joe suggested she live with Grandmother Anita. "Don't worry," Joe comforted Josie as she stood in the doorway, watching her daughter pack. "She'll be back in a week."

"I don't know," Josie said. "She's stubborn. Will you get off your high horse and at least give me a hug goodbye?" she called as Alice passed her on her way to the car.

"No," said Alice.

"Do it," Joe ordered, wheeling her around and pushing her forward.

Alice turned and endured her mother's plump arms around her, her mother's familiar stench of tobacco and violet talc and sweat and baby spit. "Goodbye, princess," Josie said. She pulled the locket off her neck and tried to loop it over Josie's head as a going away present but Josie ducked away.

"Don't worry," Joe said again. "She won't last long with Anita."

But she did. Alice was twelve when she went to live with Joe and Josie's mother, and she lasted four years. Grandmother Anita was a frail, wispy, pious old woman, given to talking to God as if God were an old lady too, complaining to Him about her ankles and bowels, taking Him with her on her daily walks to Mass, gossiping about the neighbors' lives. She scarcely noticed Alice's presence and Alice liked that; it left her free to be as "pure, renowned, and illustrious" as she chose to be. With these goals in mind, she set out to win a music scholarship to a private school where she soon became "renowned" as an "illustrious" (if friendless) student with a "pure" soprano and a killer backhand on the tennis court. Every year she grew taller and slimmer, less and less like her mother or the Grubbs. She gave thanks every day for her good Scottish looks and bright Scottish brains. Life with Anita was a mixed blessing—no more of Ern's snores or Josie's careless laughter or the boys' constant squabbling, no more airless rooms thick with alcohol and cigarettes and the stench of soiled diapers—but it wasn't perfect, for Anita had started to wander and sometimes had to be hunted down and led back home through dark city streets, and she was at least as big a liar as Josie. She told Alice, for instance, that there was no such person as *B. Sinclair,* that Josie had made him up.

"His name is on my birth certificate," Alice responded coldly. "And," holding up the tennis handbook, which she had brought with her when she left home, "it's here too."

Anita didn't even glance at the book. "Josie should have given you away when she had the chance," she said, fixing Alice with wild, dim eyes. "But you know Josie. Josie loves babies."

Alice thought about this. Josie did love babies; that was one of her problems. She loved them but she didn't know what to do with them—Jip and Bobby and Little Lloyd had always run wild, their only discipline the occasional beatings Ern roused himself to give them on the rare nights he was home. They wrecked the trailer and wrecked the yard and would have wrecked the heather Alice kept trying to grow outside her bedroom window if she hadn't screamed at them to stop. Josie never screamed. She just let things slide. She'd sit on the battered couch with the dogs and the boys cuddled around her, chuckling at some stupid television show while a dropped cigarette smoldered in the carpet and a pot of canned soup overflowed on the stove and the toilet flooded into the hallway.

That night Alice wrote Josie a long letter, demanding details. Who is *B. Sinclair*? How can I find him? Does he even know I'm alive? She never mailed the envelope. What was the point? Josie would just shrug and stick the letter in one of her romance novels somewhere and have another drink and forget about it. That was Josie's mantra anyway: "Forget about it. Give it a rest. Let it go. Never mind. Don't freak. What's the matter with you? Got a bee in your bonnet? Ants in your pants? Bats in your belfry? Relax!"

Ugh. Alice shuddered.

Alice was sixteen when she left for college, seventeen when she drove herself to the doctor and had her tubes tied, eighteen when Anita died, and nineteen when Joe was killed in a plane crash. She was twenty when she went to Scotland and twenty-two when she married a much older music professor at the University of Edinburgh. By then she had given up searching for her father's family. She had researched hundreds of Sinclairs—it apparently was one of the most common Scottish names—and though she had found handsome actors and accomplished doctors, architects, and artists, she had found no trace of a bold hero named *B* who had left his castle to marry a high school dropout and failed waitress named Josie. Discouraged to learn that many Sinclairs went by the name Sinkler, which sounded almost as bad as Grubbs, and learning further that in a clan battle with the Campbells there were so many dead Sinclairs that, as one history book put it, "the Campbells were able to cross the river without getting their feet wet," she decided to give up. Her husband was a McIntosh and she took his name. They lived in a little house near Princes' Street and when he was offered a job teaching at a music school in Florida, she did not protest. Scotland had been chilly and wet and she was not sorry to leave. She was twenty-three when she started singing professionally and twenty-five when her first collection of Gaelic ballads was released, followed soon by two more albums, which, while never best sellers, were frequently played on public radio and soon led to commercial work and voice-overs in film. Although she disliked being known as The Other Enya, Alice prospered. Her life was a good one, organized and orderly. Her husband believed her to be an orphan, raised by her grandmother, and he was surprised when he handed her the phone call from Ern. "Your mother's got the cancer," Ern said. "So if you got anything to say to her—any apology—now's the time."

"Apology?" Alice repeated, curious. "For what?"

Ern's heavy breathing on the other end of the line silenced her.

"I'll try to come," she lied, and she might have gotten away with never going back at all, but her husband, too, seemed to think she owed Josie an apology. "You have a mother you haven't seen for twenty years?" He sounded amazed. "You haven't told her about me? She doesn't know about your career?"

"We weren't a family that talked much," Alice said.

"Clearly," her husband said, and his tone was so dismissive that Alice, warned, knew it would take real effort to placate him. She made a plane reservation and was lucky only in that she arrived a day too late; Josie was already dead and the wake was already in full swing when she parked in front of the double-wide. The trailer was packed with strangers, and she made her way through the crowd gingerly, looking for someone she knew. She finally found the boys, Jip, Bobby, Little Lloyd and a new one she had never met, Chuck, huddled on the back porch sharing a joint, four small hairy men, heavily tattooed, two of them on parole for dealing meth. They didn't smile when she introduced herself or make room for her to sit beside them on the porch but they told her how Josie had died, without complaint, at peace, smiling. They wept. Alice left them and went back inside. Several of the women from the trailer park corralled her and spoke of Josie's intelligence—the books she was always reading, the way she did crossword puzzles, in ink!—and her good sense of humor, always finding something to laugh about. But one woman, standing apart, waited until everyone had drifted away and then came up to touch Alice's sleeve.

"You're *his* daughter," she said.

Alice took a deep breath. At last.

"That is, you're his legal daughter," the woman amended. "Buddy . . ."

"Buddy?" Alice repeated, her heart already sinking.

"Yes," the woman said. "Buddy Sinclair." She leaned forward confidentially. "My boyfriend at the time, and your Uncle Joe's tennis partner. Joe paid him a thousand dollars to marry Josie and give you his name so you wouldn't be a complete bastard." The woman's face was bland as she said this, and Alice, used to the stupid things music critics said, didn't blink. "We all drove up to Reno together, god that was a fun trip, and Josie and Bud had their little ceremony and shook hands and got their annulment and never saw each other again. Unfortunately," the woman paused, her eyes cold, "I never saw Buddy again either. He lost all the money at blackjack that night and disappeared."

"So I'm not a Sinclair," Alice said.

"No," the woman agreed.

"And I don't have a father."

"Oh, everyone has a father. You just don't have Buddy Sinclair as a father."

"Then who . . .?" Alice began, but the woman only winked and pressed a finger to her lips before edging out the door and disappearing into the night.

Alice spent the next hour in a daze, moving from group to group, accepting condolences. When the last mourner left she collapsed on the battered old couch and mindlessly accepted the can of beer Ern handed her. "I don't suppose you know who my father was," she said, closing her eyes in exhaustion.

"Oh sure," Ern said.

Alice sat up. She could hear her voice starting to rise, could hear the scream starting up. "Why didn't you tell me?" she managed.

"You never asked." Ern settled into the Lazy-Boy across from her and kicked off his shoes.

"I'm asking now," Alice muttered.

"So you are." Ern took a long swallow of beer and rubbed his eyes. He wasn't going to make this easy for her, Alice could tell, and she bit back her impatience. "The papers made him out to be this crazy cop killer but he was just a scared kid with a short fuse."

"My father was a murderer?" Alice interrupted.

"Well, yes, and a car thief, and a bank robber, in and out of jail since he was fourteen, but Josie loved him. You know how she was; big heart, soft spot for underdogs. They were going to get married but the idiot got into a bar fight and one thing led to another. Anyway, the cop didn't make it and neither did he." He looked at Alice. "You okay?"

She nodded.

"As I say: not a bad guy. But whew, what a temper. Josie was always worried about you, you know, those tantrums you threw. Guess that's why she treated you with kid gloves. Afraid you'd lose it if you knew the truth, blow up."

"I have never," Alice said stiffly, "lost it."

"No," Ern agreed. "And Josie didn't either. She could have had an abortion, I offered to pay for it, there was time, and she could have given you up for adoption, but no, she didn't do that either."

"She loved babies," Alice remembered.

"She loved you," Ern corrected. He rose, his empty beer can in his fist.

"What was his name?" Alice asked.

"Dwayne."

"Dwayne what?"

"Grubbs. My kid brother." Ern patted Alice's shoulder as he passed on his way to the kitchen. His hand felt so solid, so fatherly, that Alice almost reached up to cover it with her own. But she didn't. She took a sip of beer instead. It tasted terrible. She set the can down on the chipped bookshelf beside her. The shelves were crammed with Josie's ratty paperbacks and ancient grocery lists and beanie babies and smudged reading glasses and chewed dog toys and loose earrings. The tarnished locket she remembered always seeing on Josie's neck lay there too. She picked it up. It felt light as tin in her hand. Cheap. Her hand closed around it.

"Want another beer?" Ern called from the kitchen.

"No," Alice said. "Thank you." She found her purse and walked toward the door. The desert night was calm and clear and she waited to get into the rental car and drive five blocks away before parking near a dry riverbed and opening the locket.

Later she would tell her husband that she didn't know what she hoped to see inside the locket—but that would be a lie, for she still crazily hoped to find a photo of a dark haired young outlaw, a Rob Roy of the desert. What she found instead was a mirror chip. A simple mirror chip reflecting part of a face, neither Josie's face nor her own face, for the instant she saw what it was she held it far away from herself, up toward the sky, where it caught and held the moon's face, cold and white and isolated.

RAM AND DAM

SUMMERS, NOW THAT THE KIDS ARE GONE, Glen and I take the dog and drive out to the cabin on the lake. We stay all weekend. Glen has carpentry projects and the boat to keep him busy, but I don't have that much to do. The cabin doesn't have running water and we still use the outhouse—you can get used to anything, I guess—so a lot of my time is taken up with basic maintenance. I knock the cobwebs down from the rafters and wash the windows and rake the path through the oak trees and sweep up around the wood stove and do the dishes; to scour the cast iron skillet in lake water I have to squat on a limestone shelf, a chore that always makes me feel like an Osage squaw. Kidnapped! Sold to an old white man! Soon, Glen says, we'll have running water but Glen's been saying "soon" for the last twenty years and the word has lost its meaning.

I always bring work from the office and lots of library books but I rarely touch them. I swim; I take photos of the eagles; I groom the dog for ticks; I keep an eye out for copperheads; I knit. Mostly I lie out on the boat dock and watch the water. The light on the lake is ever-changing—a silky pink at dawn, a tawny tea at mid-morning (so clear you can see the gold eyes of the sunfish swirling under the pier posts), chopped liver at noon when the power boats whiz by, hammered pewter at two, tropical blue at four, a bowl of bronze as the sun sets.

Friends drop by from time to time, not as many as used to; the lake has changed, more young people now. Patti and Dodge pull their boat up to the dock to visit but Dodge can be drunk by noon and Patti has had a stroke, which makes it hard for her to talk, though she does like to sit and have her hand held. The crazy millionaire who bought up most of the south shore blows his bugle as he passes and the two gay college professors bring their guitars over to drink beer and jam with Glen on his fiddle.

In the late afternoon after everyone's left I might take a walk—the dog loves that and darts ahead of me—and we go up through the woods to the limestone bluffs to see the east side of the lake shining bright through the cedars. I always go to the very edge of the cliff and crouch to peer over to the limestone ledge beneath. The dog won't follow me there but I need to see how my wild goats are doing. There are two of them—the old ram, dead since December, but regal as a pharaoh, kneels on the ledge facing the lake, nothing left of him now but bone and horns and hanks of black and silver hair, no smell even, and his young dam stands guard beside him, sometimes turning her head to look at me with alien yellow eyes. I admire her for her loyalty and fear for her loneliness and I always say, "Stay safe" before I back away and leave.

Glen and I usually watch the sunset from the boat, motor turned off, drifting in the middle of the lake. Swallows dart and swoop around us; small mouth bass jump just out of casting reach; geese bray from the other shore. We take the iPad, so we can hear our favorite bluegrass show. Glen sips Jack Daniels from his coffee cup, I sip red wine from a thermos. We watch the sky cook—it goes from pale scrambled yolks to hot burnt apricot jam to stove-top black when the stars come out. Wild honeysuckle wafts from the shore and the lake waters offer up their good stinks of gasoline and fish. When "The Pickin' Post" is over we dock the boat and walk back up through the woods to the cabin. I cook our dinners on the camp stove—nothing fancy, just our usual standbys, spaghetti, venison chili, sometimes catfish or croppie, if Glen's caught any, and we eat on the porch by the light from the Coleman lantern. We talk—not much—I know he's worried about his prostate, though the tests show his cancer's in remission, and he knows I'm worried about our oldest, who has moved to Kansas City with yet another loser—but we spare each other our re-runs and stay still. Sometimes we share a joint. Glen plays his fiddle in the dark—"The Ashokan Farewell," my favorite, it always breaks my heart even though he flubs the same chords every time—and "The Gardenia Waltz," which, if I'm high enough, I'll dance to. Then we push the dog down to the end of the futon, check the flannel sheets for brown recluses, make love if we're lucky and fall asleep.

I do not want to dream about the wild goats but sometimes I do anyway and when I open my eyes to the night and hear the soft sounds of the woods and the lake and the owls and the hunting foxes spilling secretly, beautifully, all around us, I have to hold my breath to bite back the terror. Nothing lasts, I know that. I turn to Glen and put my arm around his shoulder, gently, so as not to wake him but once his apnea sets in I don't bother being gentle and give his back such a good smack he sits up and smacks me right back and then we both lie there and laugh until we can't laugh any more and it's time to get up, light the camp stove for coffee, and start a new day.

SUICIDE DOG

TORI WANTS TO BUY THE HOUSE in Puerto Nuevo but Stan isn't sure it's a good idea. For one thing you can't really "buy" land in Baja; you rent it, in ten year increments, and with the country as unstable as it is who knows what's going to happen in ten years. For another thing (Stan hates to say this) Tori herself is unstable. She's not crazy, Stan knows crazy, but she goes up and down and drinks too much and at twenty-nine she still believes everything everyone tells her. She believes, for instance, that the bartender setting that third pitcher of margaritas before her at the restaurant tonight is not going to charge them, that he is giving her this free out of the goodness of his heart because he likes her.

"Was she always like this?" Stan's sad eyes blur on Tori's hips, solid in white shorts, her long brown legs on tiptoe as she rises to kiss the bartender. "As a little girl did she believe in Santa Claus longer than the other kids?"

He is talking to Tori's mother, Janice, who except for the same dark hair, which she dyes, does not look a thing like her daughter; Janice wears heavy eye makeup and is so silent Stan suspects she may be deaf. Janice wishes she were. She has done nothing but listen to Stan ever since she arrived yesterday and if she had to take a test on anything he's said, she'd flunk. She sips her diet coke, and, because Stan spits a little when he talks, turns to the window overlooking the cliffs. Tori's last two boyfriends were losers but at least they were Tori's age and at least they weren't fat. "I don't remember Tori that well as a little girl," she admits.

Stan draws entwined figure-eights on the tabletop. "Is it true her father invested in abandoned gold mines?" he asks, his voice flat and rapid. "Is it true he bought an old dance hall in a ghost town and told everyone Willie Nelson would come to the opening?"

Janice nods—yes, Tori's father was a fool—and Stan leans back, satisfied, and intones something that sounds like *Alas! the inescapable genetic neurobiological architecture of parental dysfunction.* Stan uses bulky words in random order and Janice has stopped trying to sort them out. He used to be a movie director—his office in San Diego, Tori has told her, is filled with signed photographs from Stella Stevens, Barbra Streisand, and Kris Kristofferson—but now he produces a TV series about zombie surfers. He has spent the weekend waiting for his cell phone to ring and tell him whether or not the series has been renewed; that is why, he's explained, he's so jumpy. Now, reaching for the chips and gouging into the guacamole, he returns to the endlessly fascinating subject of what's wrong with Tori.

"I'm not saying BPD, all I'm saying is a definite lack of identity clarification. I mean, come on: every day a new best friend? And most of them," he shakes his head, "men?"

Janice too shakes her head; she knows better than to ask what BPD is. Yesterday Stan talked about the differences between acronyms, initialisms, and alphabetisms for almost an hour while Tori, moving swiftly from room to room, washed and folded towels, none of which Janice could find this morning after her shower.

"I love your little girl," Stan says, "and I don't want to see her get hurt."

They both watch Tori cross the crowded restaurant on her return from the bar. Tori played basketball in college and she moves like a man, every step clean and confident. You would not know she is drunk. Even with her hair yanked off her skull in spiky cornrows, she looks good, deeply tanned, slim, that splendid smile worth all the years of orthodontia. Stan's the one, Janice thinks, who is going to get hurt. Doesn't he know that? If it weren't for his money, Tori would have left him months ago. As it is, though, Janice is in no position to criticize. Stan is paying for the lobster dinner the waiter is setting down before her, Stan bought her plane ticket from Denver so she could spend this Easter weekend with them, and Stan rents the house where he and Tori have lived all winter.

This is the house Tori wants to buy, although her friend the bartender, she says, as she plops back down at their table, little braids bouncing, knows of another house, farther down the coast, that is also for sale. "Rico thinks he can get me a deal," she says. "He's going to take me to see it tomorrow."

"What time?" Despite the fact that he went to private schools and graduated from Harvard, Stan talks with his mouth full. "Because if it's in the afternoon, honey," Stan says, "I can come with you."

"Well of course you'll come with me. Mom too. You know, guys, I don't think I can eat this lobster. Does it smell funny to you? It smells like a latrine to me. It smells like the latrines at camp, Mom, where you sent me every summer to get rid of me so you could drink and screw around? That work camp?" She sets her fork down and stares across the table at Janice.

Janice continues to eat. It is important to take this from Tori, she deserves it, but does it have to happen over and over again, the same speech in the same rehearsed voice? Alas! the something something of parental dysfunction. Oh, the chores, oh, the hardships, oh, the suffering, oh, the neglect. The absent father, the abusive stepfathers, the shame of having an alcoholic mother. Janice keeps her eyes on her plate as Tori starts off on the three-margarita camp rant.

"I was practically raped every day by one of the counselors," Tori, wide-eyed, is telling the attentive Stan, "and my horse stepped on my foot and broke every bone, and I got food poisoning from the diarrhea they fed us and who came on Visitor Sunday, no one. Oh, look, is that Deb? Hey Deb! Over here!"

Deb is wiry and petite with a crooked facelift she got for two thousand dollars in Tijuana. She and the black guy with her, Felix, work in wardrobe for Fox and did a hit series with Stan a few years ago—Stan's last hit series, actually, though Stan is not worried. Things change fast in the business and if the zombies don't work out something else will. Tori cries, "Sit down, sit down!" and Stan waves to the waiter and orders another pitcher for the table, and soon Deb and Felix are joined by Sal and Deena and Meg and Gary. Almost everyone in the restaurant tonight, Janice notices, is American, and most of them, like Deb and Felix, live here.

She wonders why Tori wants to live here. The ocean, of course, but the ocean doesn't look that clean to her; there's offshore oil rigs, and the hills, even green as they are right now and bright with wild mustard, are littered with junk. The drive down to Rosarito Beach, where she and Tori went this morning, Stan yapping and flapping his hand out the window as he drove, was lined with unfinished hotels, rebar sticking out of cement blocks, burned car parts, a few villas with walls crinkle cut with shards of jagged glass. It was ugly. And Rosarito itself, where they shopped, was ugly too, a warren of shrill vendors selling cheap goods under plastic awnings. Tori led Janice to a witch woman from whom Janice obediently bought brown packets guaranteed to cure cancer, heart attacks, depression and high cholesterol, then she led her to a herbalist, from whom Janice bought vanilla, saffron, and cinnamon sticks in small firewood bundles, and then she led her to a pharmacist who filled Janice's prescriptions for Antabuse, Xanax, and Retin A without a murmur. Tori even knew the family who ran the beach palapa where they stopped for shrimp cocktails, and she sat with her smooth brown face turned up to the sun while the family's youngest daughter, standing on a wooden crate of Nehi, braided her hair, and Stan recited the entire history of zoning laws in Mexico, and Janice watched a tern fly over the waves with a songbird in its beak, followed by four shrieking seagulls who wanted it.

The house Tori wants is a bright white box with a red tile roof and blue railings. The terraces are planted with African daisies, nasturtiums, roses, and freesia; there's a swimming pool and a hot tub facing the ocean—but down the lane there's a trailer park fenced with barbed wire and the canyons behind the house are filled with tires and trash. Young women tourists are murdered on this coast every year, robbed, raped; Tori knows this but says it's no different from anywhere else: no different from summer camp was actually what she had said after margaritas last night.

The mariachi band, at Stan's weary wave, approaches and plays "Mexico Lindo y Querido," Tori's favorite song. Stan smiles at her fixedly throughout the chorus but Tori ignores him and calls to Darvid, tall and white haired, who comes in with a small dog in his arms; the dog is in a body cast, its four legs sticking out like the legs of a pinata. Darvid bends down, kisses Tori, takes the chair the waiter brings him, and pulls it close. "Your house," he breathes to Tori, "your house."

"My house?" Tori prompts, leaning forward, eyes shining.

"You know about Darvid?" Deb, bright-eyed, leans forward and whispers to Janice.

Janice nods. Yes. Darvid is a parapsychologist, he is from Israel, he has been the subject of a documentary, he is famous.

"I mean Darvid and Tori?" Deb whispers.

"Your house I was walking by this morning Tori and I had to stop." Darvid picks up one of the shrimp from the platter Stan has ordered for the table, sniffs it, and tries to feed it to the dog, who turns his head away like a cat.

"Let me?" Janice takes the dog from Darvid and stands it on her lap, where it trembles as she pets its hard skull and silky ears. "Shh shh," she soothes it.

"Watch out," Darvid says. "It is a suicide dog. Its mother killed my cat, and when I executed its mother this little one tried to run under the wheels of the RV and get killed too. I saved it because the sins of the mother et cetera." He winks at Janice who blinks back at him calmly and turns to Tori. "I had to stop outside your house because I felt the most excellent vibrations there."

"Vibrations? Did you hear that Stan? Darvid felt excellent vibrations!"

Stan throws back his head and starts to bellow "Good good *good* vibrations" in his tuneless Eastern voice. He is too smart for these people but he is not too smart for Tori. He knows she is going to get him to buy the damn house. She is going to live down here with these freeloading "friends" all week and he'll have to drive down on weekends. He can't get a divorce because his wife has breast cancer and needs his medical insurance and his oldest stepson is in college and the youngest is autistic. His life is a shit hole and there is nothing he can do about it. His phone rings.

He clamps it to his ear and says hello in a hushed voice. But no, it's only his eighty-two-year-old father, who has emphysema but still lectures in physics at the university. "I trust you are having a happy Holy Saturday," his Dad says stiffly, as mariachi starts up again in the background.

"Yes, yes," Stan mumbles. "I'm fine. And you, Daddy?"

"Can't complain," his father says, far away in Connecticut. "I renewed my pilot's license today."

"They let you take the test?"

"Of course they let me take the test," his father snaps, "I'm not the one who crash lands in our family."

Stan, humbled, listens as his father reports on the progress of his new textbook and brags about winning a tennis game with an old rival at the club. He smiles; he can't help it—he's proud of his dad. After he says goodbye and checks his messages again, he turns to Sal, who has a brother in the mob. That's a good contact to have, and Stan wants to ask him about it, but Sal, for some reason, is talking to Felix about giganticism. Stan has studied this as he has studied every known aberration. He moves his chair away from Janice and wedges between Sal and Felix. "Giganticism can't work," Stan explains. "I'll tell you why." And he begins to talk.

What Janice hears is, *If you take a worm and increase it one hundred per cent you are in essence multiplying the square of its circle cubed.* She strokes the dog. Is it true,

Janice wonders, that Stan has to have sex three times a day? She remembers last night, the sounds she heard through the guest-room wall, Stan sobbing, Tori comforting him. The dog whimpers. "He needs to pee," Darvid says. He rises and sways. They are all so drunk.

"That's all right," Janice says. "I'll take him outside." She is glad to escape with the dog in her arms and slip through the crowd to the fresh air outside. There is a fenced strip of garden along the cliff side and she sets the dog down. Moony Mexican night: it should be beautiful but isn't; the night air is laced with wafts of sewage from the restaurant. The dog walks stiffly toward a small cactus, tries to lift a leg, can't, and whimpers again. It must hurt, Janice thinks and she lifts it up so it can relieve itself, then sets it down and turns her head aside to give it privacy. How much money does Tori need for her house? And why does she need the money from Stan? Or, worse, Darvid. I could refinance my condo, Janice thinks. I could help her out. Though why? She frowns. Tori has done all right. Tori has always gotten everything she wants.

She hears a whoosh, a sharp yip, and when she turns to look the dog is gone. She circles like a dog herself, disbelieving, then steps to the fence—yes, there is a hole in it, and looks over the cliff side—yes, there is a white splotch halfway down, alive in the moonlight, and yes, it is moving.

She runs inside. Stan is busy paying the bill and Darvid is drawing something in circles on the tablecloth for Deb and Deena. She turns to the bartender. Rico will know what to do, whom to call. But Tori hears her mother stammer "dog" and "cliff" and spins toward her, eyes blazing. "You *lost* the dog?" she asks.

"I'm sorry," Janice says.

Tori wheels around, cuts through the crowd, and shoots out the restaurant door. Before Janice can reach her she has found the hole in the fence, slid through it on her stomach and is going hand over hand down the cliff.

"Hang on honey," Stan calls, pushing Darvid out of the way as he follows and before Rico can tackle him he too has stumbled toward the fence and clambered through the hole and is groping his way down the cliff in the dark. Janice kneels at the edge and peers over. The others crowd around her, jostling each other, their drinks spilling over her hair and shoulders. At first Janice sees nothing, two bobbing blobs, then she sees Tori, dog under one arm, reaching for Stan with the other arm, and as Stan struggles up, Janice in turn leans over and grabs Stan's hand, fat and sweaty. For a minute she almost giggles, thinking how funny it would be to just let them both go, but as she braces backward, she feels Rico's sinewy arms lock around her waist, then Deb's arms around Rico's waist, an entire chain of shouting friends pulling the two lovers up to solid ground, Stan's face emerging first flushed and young looking, Tori's next, stony as a little Aztec's, her eyes fixed in some mysterious triumph on her mother.

WALKING TOUR: ROHNERT PARK

THE EXERCISE BIKE MIGHT WORK for other people but after that policeman's wife on Debbie Drive lost control of hers and rammed right into the television set face first I knew it wasn't for me. She broke her jaw which was a blessing compared to that poor woman on Susie Street who was doing squats and lunges in her kitchen when she tripped and fell into her dishwasher and got stabbed to death by her steak knives; you should never load your knives tip up, I tell that to my girls Bethany and Chelsea all the time. Eighty-two percent of all accidents happen at home and the other whatever percent happens within a ten-mile radius of your home so you're not really safe anywhere. I like to see what's coming at me, so I walk. I leave every morning before Don or the girls are awake and the route I take is up Eva to Emily out to Ellen and back; it's not very scenic unless you like identical houses with identical front yards but at least I can't get lost and it does get my aerobics up.

The first house I see when I go out my front door is Barbara's, and Barbara's is not identical anymore because she just had the whole front redone for Krystal Lee's wedding. Even the grass is brand new. She ordered one of those lawns they bring in on a truck and unroll and we all went out and watched it like a movie and at the end we all clapped. Her rose bushes are new and so is that grapefruit tree; leave it to Barbara to plant something thin. The best part is that Barbara didn't have to pay for any of it; her ex-husband Lance paid for it all. He said that since Krystal Lee is his only daughter (and probably always will be after his colostomy, poor guy), why not do things right, so he gave Krystal Lee a big check and she went and gave some of the money to Barbara to fix up the house which has to be a secret from Lance because he doesn't want Barbara to get another cent. Lance thinks Krystal Lee spent it all on the wedding. She could have, too, the way things cost these days but I think she saved a little by having it at that Catholic church where the choirboy tried to crucify the homeless man, and she got a deal on the country club too because one of her bridesmaids does hair for the pro there.

It was a beautiful wedding, I will say that. Krystal Lee's colors were peach and plum, and there was a harpist and at the end they released a cage of white doves right out on the street. It turned out the priest knew the Pope, he met him in L.A. or someplace and he said the Pope said *hi* and that made Barbara feel better about the whole thing because Barbara still isn't used to the fact that Krystal Lee married an Italian. Don and I don't see what's the matter with Italians. But Barbara always has to have everything perfect.

Barbara's friend Greta Mooney who used to live next door to her liked things perfect too; you had to take your shoes off when you went over and she even had paper toilet seat liners in the bathroom. One day her husband came home and she was in her rubber gloves scrubbing the walls and he said, "Clean this up why don't you," and he took a shotgun off the mantel and blew his brains out. And after Greta went back to Germany or wherever she'd come from, this other woman moved in and she was taking a shower one day and her uterus fell out.

So that house is bad luck and the one across from it will probably be vacant soon too. See that big sign on the lawn? "I Am Earl Miller's Neighbor"? Jim Parker puts it up every morning and every night Earl Miller kicks it down. Jim and Earl used to be best friends. They both like electric trains and they bought a pool table together. Now no one knows what happened. All of a sudden these signs are going up. "For A Good Time Call Earl Miller's Wife" and then the number, the real phone number, she got the police out for that. You'd think people would try to get along but Bethany's new boyfriend Ar-Tee says that can't happen because human nature hasn't evolved since the cave age. Ar-Tee has a tattoo of Fred Flintstone on his forearm so I guess he knows, but Don and I have our fingers crossed that Bethany will break up with him soon anyway.

That lady over there says she wouldn't care who her daughters go out with, she swears she gets along with everyone, oh yes, she's so tolerant, she loves the world, she's always saying she wants more of an "ethnic mix" and how we're so "narrow" in our "world vision" here. She used to be married to a Jewish fellow and the story I heard was that he was molesting their own daughter and the girl went along with it until she found out how much prostitutes charge. The minute she started asking him for money he stopped. The girl who works at the new nail place in the mall told me about that and she told me about the man in the window over there too. Don't look. He's newly paraplegic. They think it's Lyme Disease but they don't know. They have to do more tests. His wife got him a puppy to cheer him up but when he was taking a nap one afternoon the puppy chewed one of his toes off. He didn't feel a thing because no nerves, right? and he didn't even know it was gone until his wife said, "Hey, what's that dog got in its mouth?"

They had to put the puppy to sleep because once they taste blood they change. And if you think that's sad, the girl who used to live next door? She was a year ahead of Chelsea and she was running out of Study Hall and she didn't look where she was going and she bumped into a boy running the other way and their heads hit and she died instantly but he was fine. I always think of him, the guilt he must feel every time he washes his face, and I think of that girl's parents too; they were best friends with that other couple whose baby was stolen by a cult. They still don't know what cult. For a while they thought it was that cult that pounds babies into hamburger in the name of the Devil and then they cook the baby and eat it—that's why the police can never find the evidence—but Don says that cult is only in Berkeley, thank God. We are pretty sure we had a cult living in that pink house for a while. It was a very strange arrangement, six adults, and they were always dressed up, even when they washed their cars the women wore high heels and they didn't talk to anyone except Heather Lemon when she went around with that petition to stop Dr. Wirtz from adding on to his garage.

Heather is still mad about Dr. Wirtz being the one to answer her match dot com ad but Don and I have talked about it and we think it makes sense: Heather and Dr. Wirtz are a lot alike. She's high strung and he is too; Chelsea and Bethany told us he ripped a girl's braces off a whole year early because her father missed a payment on his bill. Frankly Heather should know better—she's been fooled before. Last year this guy from Harmony dot com told her to meet him at Chevy's and he'd be the one in the cowboy hat and she turned up and he had a cowboy hat all right but he was a complete and utter midget, about three feet tall, and it was a cowboy hat from a toy store. Anyway, Heather writes this new profile saying she wants a kind, caring, professional man who is over six feet tall and this man writes back and says he's six-feet-two so they exchange photos, and Heather's is on a ski slope in sun glasses and his is on a sailboat in sun glasses so they decide to meet and they take one look at each other and start screaming right there in the restaurant. The thing is: Heather and Dr. Wirtz hate each other. They've lived next door without speaking for four and a half years; she complained to the police about his leaf blower and he poured Clorox on her rock garden. The only thing they've ever agreed on is that new fence. Don says it's the strongest fence in the neighborhood but it's not the tallest; the tallest is that one over there where the Mormon lady found the ten cats hung from the trees. She had just climbed up a ladder to put seed in her bird feeder and there they were, every cat that had been missing from the neighborhood for the last six weeks tied up with fishing line and hanging from branches and we had to chip in to hire a grief counselor for the kids they belonged to; it was even worse than the time someone went into the Finney's' backyard and shot their Yorkie with a bow and arrow to make it stop barking.

The sickest thing that's ever happened in those trees though is the rapist who tried to catch the seven-year-old girl by dropping dollar bills along the sidewalk. She followed the trail until she got into the trees and he grabbed her. Luckily she remembered to scream like they teach you in school these days and she ran into the street and this is the worst part because no one stopped to help her until her own father drove by on his way home from work and the first thing he said was, "Where'd you get all that money?"

"We're just too used to crazies," Don says. I remember that lady on Della Court who started out giving regular garage sales, once a month, like other people, and then something happened, she got addicted, and she had to have them all the time and pretty soon she was selling things like her kids' bunk beds when they were in school and their ferret cages with the ferrets still in them and her husband's guns and some of his power tools; I think she even tried to sell the Jeep before they got her into treatment. I always think of her carrying all her living room furniture out to the street by herself every morning but of course she was harmless. Not all of them are. I know for my own peace of mind I won't take a shower when I'm alone in the house. When Don's at work and the girls are at school, I won't even go upstairs. I just put the folded laundry on the landing and when everyone's home I carry it up and make a lot of noise so if anyone is in the closet they have plenty of time to get out. They never did catch that rapist, after all, and there are plenty of others just like him out there. I always think of our Pastor, ex-Pastor that is. Even Don won't go to his church any more. Here he was, this perfect Pastor, always holding prayer circles to cure people of their homosexuality and all the time he had AIDS and a whole double life like that young banker in Santa Rosa who drowned the call girl in the hot tub while his wife was on a Girl Scouts overnight with their two little daughters. Don misses church, I know, and being an usher, and I hope he finds something soon because he's been in a terrible mood since Krystal Lee's wedding. At first he said it was a toothache but finally he told me the truth: Lance didn't recognize him in the reception line. Don has put on some weight lately but he hasn't changed that much. Lance is the one who's changed. I don't know what he's done but he's gotten so handsome; maybe it's the suffering he's been through but even Bethany and Chelsea noticed he looked better than he did when he lived across the street from us. He was wearing a royal blue tux at the wedding and if there was a bag inside I couldn't smell it and I'm usually sensitive to things like that. He didn't talk to Barbara of course but did dance with Krystal Lee and they looked so sweet together I wanted to cry.

The other one who danced was this girl Shandora who knows Krystal Lee from modeling school, and what she did was dirty dancing, I don't know what else you'd call it. I haven't seen it outside the movie but that's what it was. And there was this one man who started dancing with her. He was doing it too. I mean, he was ready to eat her up right there on the dance floor. And she was ready to let him. When the band took a break they went outside toward the cars and Don and I looked at each other and thought uh-oh and then she ran back in and the man was right behind her and he was even drunker than before and he was going to get her, I mean the Italians had to hold him back, he was really going to get her, right in front of everyone. We all made a circle around her until they locked him in a car. Then Barbara took Shandora home with her and she slept on Barbara's bathroom floor—I know that doesn't sound so great but you should see Barbara's bathroom since she had it redone with Lance's money—and Shandora had a blanket near the bidet in case she needed it and I guess she did because the carpet was being steam cleaned when I went over to have coffee with Barbara last week.

And that was when Barbara told me this . . . thing . . . this really strange thing. She said that after she got Shandora home she called Heather Lemon and Heather came over and the two of them examined Shandora to see if she'd had sex with the man. I mean, they *examined* her. They took off her clothes and pried her legs open and looked up inside her with a flashlight. Shandora was passed out the whole time. Heather's a paralegal and Barbara said if they found any sign of sexual activity, sperm or what have you, they were going to sue that man for date rape. Lucky for him they didn't find anything. Shandora is still over there, in Krystal Lee's old room, and Barbara said she is thinking of moving in permanently. I wouldn't like someone like that living in my house. Also, I think: What is rape? Isn't what Barbara and Heather Lemon did to her rape?

I am puzzled by the whole situation. Yesterday I said to Don, if someone examined me they'd find out I haven't had sex since 1998 but I don't think Don took the hint. He was reading this diet book Bethany and Chelsea gave him for Father's Day; he wants to do this new one, it's all meat and potatoes, nothing else, which is basically all he eats anyway. He's in a rut and I guess I'm in one, too. Every morning I wake up early and lie in bed worrying that nothing will ever happen except I'll get older and the girls will grow up and go away and Barbara will always have better things than I do and Don will die from high cholesterol and I'll be all alone. And then—I can't help it—I imagine Don's funeral and what I'll wear and how Lance will stay after the service and say he's always been in love with me and I'll have to think: Do I really want to get married again? To someone with physical problems? But once the sun's up and I'm on my walk I forget my worries and by the time I pass this house (this is where the girl lived whose breast implants froze when she went on a ski trip), and that house (that's where they had to hire an exorcist because the television turned on to "Jeopardy" every day by itself)—I feel better. There is nothing like fresh air to put things in perspective.

WILLOW SPRINGS EDITIONS IS A SMALL LITERARY PRESS housed in Eastern Washington University's Inland Northwest Center for Writers, in Spokane. The staff of Willow Springs Editions is comprised mostly of creative writing graduate and undergraduate students under the direction of Christopher Howell. As part of an internship for which they receive college credit, the students get hands-on experience in every phase of the publishing process. Willow Springs Editions staff oversees the annual Spokane Prize for Fiction competition. They also publish annually one surrealist poetry chapbook.

Willow Springs Editions staff who contributed to this book include Derek Annis, Shay Aurand, LeAnn Bjerken, Jess Bryant, Twila Colley, Jamie Cotner, Vladislav Frederick, Paulina Garcia, Erin Greene, Marie Hoffman, Dorian Karahalios, Ryan Lowe, Ben Murray, Ian Parker, Austin Prettyman, Kati Stunkard, Kyle Thiele, Nicholas Thomas, Lareign Ward, Lexi Watkins and Caitlin Wheeler.

THE SPOKANE PRIZE FOR SHORT FICTION

THE SPOKANE PRIZE FOR SHORT FICTION is made possible through the partnership of Lost Horse Press and Willow Springs Editions. Based in Sandpoint, Idaho, Lost Horse Press is a 501(c)(3) nonprofit, independent press that publishes the works of established as well as emerging poets, and makes available wonderfully unique contemporary literature through cultural, educational and publishing programs and activities. This and other Lost Horse Press titles may be viewed online at www.losthorsepress.org. Previous winners of the Spokane Prize for Short Fiction as well as Willow Springs Editions chapbooks can be viewed at http://sites.ewu.edu/wseditions.